LIVE BY IT

DIE BY IT

ICE MONEY

LIVE BY IT, DIE BY IT

Printed in the United States of America.

ISBN: 978-0-9992646-7-6

TABLE OF CONTENTS

ABOUT THE AUTHOR

Ice Money is a native of Milwaukee, Wisconsin. He is a proud father of one, an entrepreneur, the Vice President of So Geeked Records, a man with a business mind, he's charismatic, versatile, a good basketball player, and he loves music and his family.

Growing up in poverty and a city of high crime, he would eventually find himself heading down that road. Trouble with the law sent his life spiraling out of control, but through incarceration, which he considers both a curse and a blessing, he has found another talent that he didn't even know he had: writing books.

He regrets none of his life experiences because they have made him who he is today. Instead, he uses his experiences as fuel to succeed and always strives to reach his full potential.

Ice Money is a writer of urban fiction and erotica at this point. However, his books are in no way meant to encourage people to adopt a criminal's path in life. They are lessons and entertainment, simply the reality of what takes place in many inner-city ghettos and hoods around America. Therefore, enjoy his work as he expresses his imagination on a level that will keep you turning pages and wanting more.

Ice Money is currently incarcerated, but like most things, that will soon come to an end. Until then, he will continue to put out real urban street literature for your entertainment.

Also, be on the lookout for some of So Geeked Records hottest artists: Party Boi, Amazin, Young Major, Cheddar Boy, King Los, and many more.

ACKNOWLEDGEMENT

To my son AP3, every father has expectations for his child when they are first born, so when the first time I held you in my arms and I looked at you and you looked me, I knew you would do wonderful things in your life. I mean, I wanted to teach you everything I knew, from A to Z so you'd be prepared for this world and what life has to offer, but we know what happened and everything I would've loved to be there for, I missed out on. However, you and I have maintained a very close father son relationship over the years, and I have watched you grow into a mature young man. I like to listen when you give me the play by play about any and everything you have going on. I know you're still in High School right now, but I want you to know that you have superseded my expectations thus far son. I am extremely proud of you in all facets, know that! It's almost over, and it's me and you, keep doing what you're doing and working hard in your books as well as on your game, and I'll see you on the court. I love you son always, know that!!!

CHAPTER ONE

ichie Rich sat with his seat back behind tints in the parking lot of Walmart on East Capital in his outrageous purple 1996 Chevy Impala SS sitting on chrome 26" Rucci rims. Yo Gotti's new CD "The Art of Hustle" bumped low out of his four twelves from the trunk.

Checking his mirrors, he had his phone in his hand and his F&N pistol on his lap. He had come a long way in the game, but the events that led him to this point plagued his thoughts.

A year ago, he had lost both of his parents in a tragic car accident and no matter what, that would always be an open scar on his heart. He was fortunate enough to be raised by both parents and they were hard working responsible people who always put him and his two brothers first.

Richie Rich was the oldest at 24 years old, then his brother RJ who was 22, and their youngest brother whose name is Jacoby was 16.

Richie Rich felt like since he was the oldest, it was his duty to take care of his younger brothers. But his Aunt took Jacoby in because she did not like the lifestyle Richie chose, especially since he had a felony under his belt and served two years in a juvenile detention facility when he was 16 to 18 years old for a drug charge. His Aunt even went as far as to bird feed him the insurance money that his parents left for him and his brothers. Now, no monetary gain could replace his parents, but the insurance money was to give them a cushion, and his Aunt was trying to be judge and jury, She probably put their money into the collection plate every Sunday as far as he knew.

He wasn't tripping though. She gave him $15,000 about 8 months ago and he bought a half kilo and didn't look back.

Jacoby was one of Wisconsin's premiere basketball players. He was a beast. And RJ, well, Richie felt like he was trying to live in his shadows. He was always doing too much and talking too much. He was family with a little bit of hustle in him, but Richie didn't think he possessed what it took to get some real money on the mean streets of Milwaukee Wisconsin, so he kinda gave him the cold shoulder.

Richie Rich's thoughts were interrupted by a knock at the window.

"So, you not gon' open the door?" Jamillah said with attitude. She was Richie Rich's ride or die. He met her during his freshman year of high school, she was his first love. He broke her virginity, and when he went to do his stint in the detention center, she made sure that he was able to call her. She wrote him every day, and if not, then every other day. She would often ride up to see him with Richie Rich's parents. Honestly, he was shocked that she held it down like that because it is certainly a rarity that women do that for their men while they are in prison, especially with her being so young. So, when he got out, he tried to give her everything in his grasp. She was a simple woman, so it didn't take much to please her.

"You betta not break my door," he smiled while unlocking the door.

"Or what nigga," she said while getting in and trying to push his head. But Richie Rich saw it coming and moved out the way.

"Chill out, that's how you gon' treat me when I been sitting out here for an hour missing all type of action waiting on you."

"No baby," she said and leaned in for her hug and kiss, then he reached around and cuffed the half of her ass that raised up in the seat. "You know them lines in Walmart be long azz hell, especially since it's the first of the month. The chick that had to relieve me was late, and then I had to count my drawer after that. It was fucked up today," she added while adjusting in her seat.

"Well, you ain't gon' have to worry about that pretty soon, you finna be outta there. I really haven't been stressing you over it because I know that you like to be busy every day. You need to let me open you up a hair salon. All those people's braids you be doing for free, you might as well get paid," Richie Rich said while pulling the gearshift into drive and pulling off.

"Boy, I like my job and doing hair is a hobby of mine," she said and smiled. "What did they say about my car?" she continued.

"You need new brake pads, a front-end alignment, and new tires. It should be done by tomorrow, at least that's what the mechanic said," Richie Rich said as he slid the pistol under his armrest. "I don't know why you just didn't take the truck anyway," he added

"I'm not driving that big azz truck," she retorted

"Whatever, you want me to drop you off at home?" he asked

"Naw, Keisha wants me to come over there, so drop me off over her house."

"For what? To do some free azz hair?"

"Smt, boy just take me over there," she said after smacking her teeth. Richie Rich was about to respond until his phone rang. He looked at the caller ID and saw that it was RJ.

What the fuck this nigga want? Richie Rich answered, "What up?"

"Bro, they got the gamble crackin' over here, niggas shootin' that money," RJ said, putting emphasis on the word money.

"Oh yeah, where you at?"

"In the back of the gas station in the hood."

"Tray five?"

"Yeah."

"I'm on my way," Richie said then hung up. "Listen baby, I'm finna pull up in the hood. You take the car and go do what you gotta do, and then drive yourself to the crib. Text me when you get there, when you leave, and when you get home, aight?"

"Yeah, I got you baby."

"Aight," Richie Rich said then hit a couple notches on the volume button. "Down in the DM" thumped out of the speakers as he moved through traffic base lining. After answering a couple calls and serving some of his actions, he pulled up in 36th and Garfield and turned the music down.

"Aight baby, make sure you watching those mirrors. You got yo tramp on you?"

"Yeah, it's in my purse."

"Okay, make sure you call me or text me, I'll see you when I get to the crib later," he said, then leaned over and kissed her two times on the lips. Jamillah was one of the bright spots in his troubled life. He learned that every man needs a woman when his life is a mess because the Queen protects the King just like in the game of chess. He'd never forget something she wrote to him in one of her numerous letters while he was incarcerated. She told him that she would never leave him alone, he is her king. Missing him is her hobby, caring for him is her job, making him happy is her duty, and loving him is her heart. That was the most loving thing that anyone had ever told him. They had grown so close that she was closer to him than his own jugular vein, and he knew she was the one for him and he would cherish and honor her for the rest of his days.

"Be safe out there baby, I love you," she said after their kiss.

"I love you too," he said before stuffing the F&N down in his waistband, grabbing his phone, and getting out of the car. "Don't forget what I said," he reminded her as she scooted to the driver's seat.

"I won't," she said, closing the door and pulling off. Richie Rich walked east across the street, through the gang way, and into the alley behind the gas station on 35th and Garfield where he saw about 20 to 30 people huddled up around the dice game.

Walking toward the gamble, he spotted RJ coming in his direction.

"What up, you ain't gettin' down?" Richie asked

"Hell Naw, you know I ain't too good on them muthafuckas, I was just watching Chauncey square azz."

"Where he at?"

"On the dice passing on they azz too," RJ admitted

"What they shootin'?"

"Shit everything from what I been seeing."

"You got a pole on you?"

"Nope"

"Well hold the ratchet, and if shit get hectic, you betta bust this muthafucka too, and hold my sack too," Richie Rich said passing him a little under two zips.

"You already know I'mma drop a nigga first sign of bullshit, I'm too trained to go, believe that," RJ jacked while stuffing the gun in his pocket and the dope in his waistband as he and Richie made it to the circle. The only reason he gave RJ the pistol is because he was about to be on the dice shooting and he didn't wanna miss anything while he was getting money, so with RJ just standing on the side line, he figured he had a better vantage point to see some shit before it happened and bail him outta trouble if any came his way. Besides, with money and dice in his hands it would've been too hard to try to pull out a pistol if shit hit the fan.

"Let me get in here, I got a few dollars to lose," Richie said while pulling the $3,200 from his pocket. The knot of 10's, 20's, 50's, and a few 100's looked more than what it actually was, so you know all the wolves around were anxious to get him into the gamble so they could take a look at him. "Who next on the fade?" he continued

"Me," some lil nigga that Richie Rich had seen around from time to time on 37th and Lloyd. Richie looked and saw the few hundred he had in his hand, so he had an idea.

"I'll give you these four fifty-dollar bills to buy your fade," he bargained

"Shit bet!" lil dude said accepting the $200 dollars. Richie Rich smiled. He knew his ice cold reroll was the shit, so he'd get that back and some more.

Richie looked at Chauncey who was his best friend. He had met Chauncey while he was in detention, and he was his right-hand man. When they were locked up, they became super close. They ate together, fought together, played basketball together, and formed a solid brotherhood that transitioned to the streets where they were now getting money. The knot in Chauncey's hand let Richie know that he was feeling it today, and that was evident when he just hit his point and picked up the two $50's.

Chauncey looked at Richie and smiled. He was sure he was hot today on the dice, but he knew Richie had the type of roll that could break a dice game up, so he wanted to get him in. They had done this a thousand times before, and each knew exactly what to do.

Chauncey picked the dice up and shook 'em. "Shoot a hunnid, hit for a hunnid," he said dropping his money as Richie dropped $200. Chauncey rolled the dice and Richie caught 'em.

"You ain finna get it like that," Richie said knocking the dice outta the way as soon as they landed.

"Don't get spooked now, you saw that seven winking."

"Well hit it again then."

"What? I hit for another hunnid," Chauncey said dropping his money while Richie dropped his. Chauncey shook the dice and rolled 'em with a snap. "Seven dice," he added as he rolled a five. "I nine to five for a hunnid," he continued while dropping the money and Richie dropped his. This was all a part of their master plan. They had to raise the stakes, so that it wouldn't take too long to break everybody once Richie got on the dice.

Picking up the dice, Chauncey rolled with a snap, and Richie caught 'em. Picking 'em up again, Chauncey shook 'em and rolled only to end up crapping out. The plan was really in play now once Richie got on the dice.

Scooping up the money, Richie then left $300 dollars down. "Shoot $150, hit $150," he said while standing up and shaking the dice. Richie knew a couple of people in the circle, and of course he wanted all of their money, but he mainly wanted the dude's money with the big boy white buff Cartier glasses with the diamonds in them, and Berluti Ferro suede and leather high top sneakers. Richie knew those shoes were worth over $1,500, and he had a Patek watch on his wrist. He looked like money, and Richie wanted it, so he gave some urge to not only him, but anybody out there who thought they were ready for him.

"Who fadin', all you niggas out here with yays on with D's in 'em, and all kinda exclusive gear on, let me find out y'all cappin' and blew all y'all money to look good," he said and looked the dude square in the eyes.

"Who you talkin' too?" the dude asked

"Whoever felt like I was talking to them. I ain't scared to shoot no money. On my nigga, I'll call my woman right now and have her bring twenty right now, all blue faces," he replied, making dude feel some type of way.

"My name Cash fam and I got it. I can have my bitch bring twenty too. But I'd prefer you to call yours and run that."

"What they hittin' fo then?" Richie asked ready to get to it.

"Shoot $500, hit $500 if that ain't too much for you while you jackin' about this money shit," Cash said while digging in his pocket and pulling out an extra-large wad of money.

'Got 'em' Richie thought to himself. Pride was a muthafucka and Richie could tell Cash was very prideful and he was ready to take advantage of that fully. "I ain't jackin' at all, and that certainly ain't too much," Richie said dropping $700 on the ground with a smile. Shaking the dice, he rolled 'em and hit snake eyes. "I'm coming back," Richie added while dropping his money before he picked the dice up.

"I knew you wasn't on shit, matter of fact, shoot a gee, hit a gee," Cash said

"Bet," Richie said dropping another gee, knowing he was about to trim his azz. "Anybody else wanna bet I don't hit?" he added while looking through the crowd.

"I say you don't hit for a hunnid," Steve said. He was off 34th and North

"Me too," Pimp said. He was a gambling muthafucka, but so was Richie, and dice was something he rarely ever lost at.

"It's good, drop it," Richie said while putting two more hundred on the ground. Then, Richie switched the dice from his right hand to his left hand and shook 'em. A couple of people noticed that he switched hands and knew he was finna get on bidness. Shaking the dice, Richie let 'em roll out of his hand and snapped his fingers. "Get 'em girls," he continued as the dice stopped on #5, and the other spun til it landed on #1. "I straight six to anybody for this last little $400," he added

"Bet," came from somebody in the crowd but before they could step up.

"Fader got that bet," Cash said and dropped four $100 dollar bills on the ground. Richie dropped his, picked the dice up in his left hand, and shook 'em. Then he rolled 'em out.

"Get 'em girls," Richie said and snapped his fingers. He rolled double #2's.

"That's an indicator," he added while picking up the dice and shaking them again. Then he rolled 'em. "Get 'em hoes," he said, and both dice landed on double #3's.

"I told you that was an indicator. You should've caught them, y'all know I'm off the tray's," he continued while picking up his money and leaving two gees on the ground.

"Shoot that shit nigga," Cash said dropping the money as Richie placed a few more bets then shook 'em in his left hand a couple times before he shot 'em out.

"Get 'em hoes," he said and a #5 and #6 showed on the dice. Richie quickly scooped up the money and left two gees down.

"Shoot," Cash said and dropped his money. Richie then got a few more non-believers to side bet, then he shook 'em, and let 'em roll.

"Get right hoes," he said as he rolled his point of ten. After a few more rolls he hit that point as well. He was too turnt up now, and for the next hour Richie hit sevens and elevens. Point after point, everybody besides the people whose money he was taking were geeked up. RJ and Chauncey just looked on. They had seen him do this several times before.

Richie had received texts from Jamillah that she made it to her friend's house, that she left her friend's house, and that she made it to their home, and he was still at it. Not to mention all the money he missed from his clientele while being back there gambling.

Richie became tired and was sweating profusely. He had all his pockets stuffed to capacity, so he had started handing money to Chauncey to hold. Cash had called his girl two separate times. First, she brought 10 gees, and when Richie ran through that, he called her back and she brought 20 gees, but Richie took all of that as well. Now he was ready to go get into something else.

"I'm done bro," Richie said leaving the dice on the ground after he hit his last point and scooped up his money.

"Shoot that shit nigga, that lil shit you won from me ain't break me," Cash said throwing two gees down.

"You right, it ain't shit, but I got other shit to do," Richie reasoned, but Cash wasn't tryna hear that.

"Shoot five gees then," Cash said dropping three more gees down. As tempting as that was, Richie knew he had to get up outta there after winning all of that money. He was on the Tray's and as much as he loved his hood, he knew it was shiesty as hell too, and he didn't wanna become a walking lic.

"I'm good, I'll slide through tomorrow or something and see what's hat-nen."

Richie said while backing away from the crowd.

"Bitch azz nigga I wasn't askin'. I said shoot that shit," Cash replied, making the situation go in a whole different direction.

"Hold on nigga, you betta watch yo muthafuckin' mouth. Don't yell at me, yell at yo bitch," Richie retorted, and peeped RJ slide his hand in his pocket were the pistol was.

"I ain't tryna hear that bitch azz nigga. Now shoot that shit or I'mma shoot you," Cash said pulling out a .40 and cocking it. Richie's heart rate quickened, and he was in immediate danger when Cash pulled his weapon. Glancing over to RJ, Richie wondered what the fuck he was thinking. Cash had pulled a pistol and threatened to pop him, so all that player shit went out the window, he needed RJ to pop Cash before Cash popped him. "Nigga you heard what the fuck I said, matter of fact, run all that shit you got in them pockets," he continued before pointing the pistol at Richie who was backing up shaking his head no. Then three shots rang out in a loud blast. Richie closed his eyes knowing he had been shot. Feeling nothing, he opened his eyes to see Cash falling down face first as the crowd started to disburse. Richie then saw Chauncey standing there holding his pole.

Chauncey waved his gun to Richie as if to say come on, and Richie snapped out of his trance, and ran behind Chauncey with RJ right behind him. They ran through cut after cut, through the alley, and across the street until they ended up on 39th and Garfield.

Going in the house using the back door, they made it to the living room, and caught their breath, then Richie turnt up.

"Where my heat and my dope at?" he asked RJ still pissed at him. RJ didn't say anything, he dug in his pocket, passed Richie his F&N, then he patted his waistline, checked his pockets, looked at Richie, and said, "Bro, the dope must've fell out while we was running." Richie had heard enough as he cocked back and hit RJ in the jaw, knocking him to the floor as Chauncey hopped between them.

"Hoe azz nigga, not only did you lose my work, but you was finna let a nigga kill me. I told yo soft azz if shit get hectic to let that bitch ride and what yo hoe azz say, I'mma drop a nigga quick, I'm trained to go, and all that weak azz shit. You froze right the fuck up in the middle of that action, nigga I should..." Richie said, trying to get at him, but Chauncey held him back.

"I ain't think it was gon' go that far," RJ said while getting up off the floor holding his jaw.

"You ain't think it was gon' go that far? The nigga upped a pistol on me and was about to do me if it wasn't for Chauncey. What he had to do, pop me once so you know it was serious? And you wonder why I don't fuck wit you like that, you always fucking something up. I'd be the one laying behind that station right now if it was up to you, I can't even look at you right now," Richie said with disgust

"My nigga chill, you know he ain't ready for that type of shit, but I got you always," Chauncey said.

"I know, good lookin' too."

"No doubt," Chauncey said shaking his hand.

"I'm finna get up outta here, before the law be everywhere," Richie said.

"Me too, I gotta go dump this pistol, get this gun powder off me, and change clothes."

"You want me to drop you off?"

"Naw, I gotta rental parked on 40th, here go yo bread too from the gamble."

"Keep it, just get at me in the morning bro, or if you need me before then," Richie said, tucking his pistol in his waistband.

"Fo sho," Chauncey said. As they walked, Richie turned back and shot RJ a stare that was colder than January before he left.

Leaving out of the back door, Chauncey hit the cut, and Richie hit the alarm on his Yukon that was parked in the back of the spot and pulled off heading home using the back streets. He couldn't believe RJ didn't pull that pistol out and pop Cash. He knew from that point on that he could never put that much trust in him again.

Stupid azz nigga, Richie thought to himself as he made a left turn.

CHAPTER TWO

*R*ichie entered the home that he shared with Jamillah and pressed the code to activate the home security system. While walking down the hallway to their bedroom, his mind was still racing about the events that took place earlier tonight. His life had literally flashed before his eyes, and his brother almost let a nigga shoot him. It was just mind boggling to him and all he wanted to do now at that point was get as close as he could to the one that he loved the most. He knew that no matter what, she would always have his back.

Entering their room, he spotted Jamillah standing in the mirror combing her hair out and wrapped in a towel. Apparently, she had just gotten out of the shower.

"Oh, hey baby," she said as she continued doing what she was doing. Upon hearing no response, she turned around to see Richie pulling stack after stack of money out of his pockets, then he placed his pistol and phone on the dresser.

"What's wrong with y..." she tried to speak but was cut off by him grabbing her, hugging her, and kissing her passionately. As their tongues explored each other's mouths, Richie's hands explored her body as he cuffed two handfuls of her plentiful ass and squeezed her cheeks.

Bringing their kiss to a halt, Richie stepped back and removed the towel from her body and licked his lips. Her body always did something to him every time he seen her naked, and he was becoming more and more aroused with each second that passed.

Turning her over, he helped her to get on all fours on their bed, and then he slapped her ass.

"Ummm," Jamillah moaned as Richie grabbed both of her ass cheeks in his hands and wiggled them, then he bit her softly on her ass cheek causing another soft moan to escape her lips. Spreading her ass cheeks, he put his face in between them and licked her winking ass hole making sure that it was saliva soaked, then he blew on it softly before pushing his tongue in her ass hole. Pulling his tongue out, he slid his finger in there. While his finger was in there twirling in a circular motion, he buried his face in her pussy and slopped it up with his tongue while slurping and licking inside of her sweet nectar. Taking his other hand, he stuck those fingers in her pussy as he continued to lick and suck from back and forth between her ass and her pussy as his fingers were still in motion. Satisfied with that, he flipped her over onto her back and put his fingers back in the same places as he licked and sucked hard on her clit.

"Oohh baby, I'm finna cum," she said while holding the back of his head in her hands as he feasted hard on her clit while increasing the speed of his twirling fingers that were in her ass and pussy. "Ohh Richie! Ahh!" she moaned as she came in his mouth. Richie didn't let anything fall as he slurped, licked, sucked, and swallowed everything she had to offer after he removed his fingers.

Moving up toward her, he tongue kissed her so that she could taste her sweet juices off of his tongue and lips. Then he moved down, grabbed her breasts, and squeezed them softly.

Putting her pierced nipple in his mouth, he sucked on it as he massaged the other one. Then he switched to do the other one before pushing them both together and sucking on them both.

After that, he stood up, took off his shoes, and removed his shirt, pants, and boxers. Opening her legs, he got in between them, grabbed his fully erect member and rubbed it through her dripping wet pussy to moisten the head. Then he slapped his dick on top of the pussy a few times before he slid in halfway, took it back out, slapped it again a few more times, and slid back in ready to put in work.

"Yes, daddy yassss!" she groaned encouraging him that she liked what he was doing to her body. Richie went in inch by inch deep as he felt her grabbing at his back. Her pussy muscles were gripping him like a sock around a foot. After adjusting to his size, she spread her legs wider, and he put them on his shoulders and beat her pussy up as she went crazy. "Ah fuck...beat it up baby, ahhhh, owww...shit," she moaned as she started climbing an invisible ladder and reaching for shit that wasn't even there.

Richie leaned down and kissed her as he slowed his pace down to a slower circular motion of the hips, then he sucked on her titties as she held them for him.

Richie and Jamillah were great lovers to each other. They were moving in a rhythmically tone like they were listening to music, but the only sounds that could be heard was skin clapping, moaning, groaning, and grunting.

Richie could feel her getting more wet, so he started to pick his pace back up as her body relayed the message to him through her actions that she was enjoying the pleasure and so was he.

"Ohh...I'm...Cummin!" she yelled as Richie looked down and saw a thin white film coat his dick from her orgasm. He smiled knowing he was giving his woman the pleasure she desired and deserved.

Pulling out, he laid next to her, and didn't have to say a word. She knew exactly what he wanted, what she always did to him since they were younger, he wanted her to ride the dick.

Jamillah got up, threw her leg across him as he watched her titties bounce, shake, and jiggle. She then reached for his member, held it in place, slid it into herself, and sat all the way down on it as he gripped each of her ass cheeks with both hands. Jamillah then leaned over and kissed him passionately before she started to grind, twirl, and bounce on his dick while he sucked on her titties. She was riding him like a horse and she was the cowgirl when all of a sudden Richie felt a strong surge shoot through his nut sack, making its way to the top and signaling that his nut was about to explode. So was Jamillah's as she slid up and really started to put her back into it. They were both in a sexual trance as they both hollered.

"Ohh shit!" Jamillah yelled.

"Arraaghh!" Richie grunted as they both came in unison, something they both did together often.

Jamillah laid on top of his chest as they were panting after the great sex session that just went down. She stayed up there until his dick went flaccid and came out of her. Then she got up, slid on her slippers, and walked toward the door.

"Where you goin'?" Richie asked.

"To use the bathroom and get something to drink. I need to replace the fluids that you just sucked outta me," she said as they shared a giggle.

"Bring me something back too."

"I got you," she said and left the room. Before she even made it back, Richie was sound asleep.

*****

The next morning, Richie Rich awoke to his and ringing cellphone and answered it.

"What up?"

"You good my dude?" Chauncey asked.

"I'm good, thanks to you."

"Come on bro, you already know, but we ain't gon' even go there on this line."

"You right, what you on today?"

"Shit, I just rode through the nine a few times tryna see what up. The streets silent, so I'm finna get to the paper," Chauncey said, letting him know that he been through 39th street where their spot was and there was no sign of the law, which was always a good thing.

"Aight, I'mma meet you at the tip in an hour," Richie said.

"Cool, love."

"Love bro," Richie said, ending the call. Placing the phone back on the dresser, he turned to see Jamillah sitting with her back against the headboard. Fully clothed, she was watching reruns of Love & Hip-Hop Atlanta.

Turning to meet his eyes, she stared at him with a blank look on her face.

"Damn baby, what's up?" he asked while sitting up and removing the covers from his naked body.

"Waiting on you to tell me what's going on with you," she responded.

"Why would you think something is wrong with me?" he said while getting outta bed and sliding on a pair of basketball shorts and his Air Jordan slippers.

"Because I know something's wrong. Last night you fucked me like you was never going to see me again," she said. That instantly hit him in the gut, so he didn't respond, he just walked out of the room to the bathroom with her coming in hot on his tail. Richie grabbed his toothbrush, put some Colgate on it, hit it with a little water, and started brushing. "Well?" she added.

"Well what?" he said after spitting toothpaste in the toilet.

"Richie, I know you better than anybody, so don't play with my intelligence, I know something is bothering you, and that phone call with Chauncey sounded very suspicious, so if you're in some type of trouble you need to let me know that, and I'mma help you in any way I can," she said with sincerity while watching him rinse out his mouth and was his face. "Fuck it, don't tell me shit then, I'm gon' from it," she continued and walked off after waiting a brief moment for him to say something which he didn't.

Richie shook his head. He knew in order to keep their foundation solid, he had to reveal a few things just to let her know that he wouldn't hide anything from her. Jamillah was his ride or die. She would do anything for him, and he knew that. She had proven that time after time. She had stuffed his sack so many times. When they would get pulled over, she would hold his heat, and bust it if he told her to. After all, it was her that held him down during his two-year stint in Detention, so with that alone, he knew she deserved to be treated better than what he was showing her. How could he call himself a real nigga if he wasn't true to the one who he was trying to build his empire with? He couldn't. Besides, she already knew too much about everything, and he fully trusted her more than anyone. She never gave him a reason not to.

Hanging his towel back on the rack, he drained the dragon, washed his hands, and hopped in the shower.

Ten minutes later, he hopped out, dried off, wrapped the towel around his waist, slid into his slippers, and made his way back to the room.

Walking in through the door, he saw Jamillah sitting on the bed looking too pissed off, like a child whose Mother said they couldn't go outside and play on a nice summer day. We all know how mad that is. Seeing the money that he threw on the floor on the dresser neatly stacked, he said, "How much was it?" He knew she counted it already, but she didn't reply. "So you not going to leave this alone?" he asked as he handled his hygiene, but she ignored him again. "So you don't hear me talking to you?" he added while putting on his boxer briefs.

"You wasn't tryna say shit when I wanted to talk," she snapped at him. Jamillah was a beautiful woman and she had a hair trigger attitude, and Richie knew this, so he stayed poised. He was way too clever to engage in an argument with his woman. That was always a conundrum that he didn't wanna deal with. He had mastered this game a long time ago, so he flipped the script on her knowing the only thing a woman wants to hear is that she is right even though she may not be, there's nothing wrong with making them think that you were wrong.

"You right baby, and I was wrong for that. I realized that while I was in the shower, so as you man, I respect you. I came to correct it, do you still wanna talk about it?" he reasoned.

"Yes, I would like that," she said totally switching up her attitude. *I still got it*, Richie thought to himself.

"So, what's up?" he said, beating around the bush as she smacked her teeth. "Okay okay, but you betta not repeat shit I'm finna tell you and I mean it," he spoke sternly as he sat next to her on the bed.

"I never repeated anything you told me or anything I saw, and you know that," she reminded him. With that, Richie told her about the events that took place after she dropped him off yesterday.

"So, RJ was just gon' stand there and let that nigga shoot you? What the fuck was he on? No wonder why you whopped his azz. Chauncey should've let you too," Jamillah stated.

"Right, if it wasn't for Chauncey...I might not be here right now," Richie said as Jamillah became emotional over the thought of losing him.

"Richie, what the fuck am I supposed to do if something's happens to you? I love you baby and I don't wanna know what it's like not to have you," she said while wiping her tears as Richie hugged her tightly.

"I love you too baby. The things we go through in life equip us to be better suited for our future, so I take this as a learning experience, and I definitely learned something from this."

"What did you learn baby?"

"Not to let RJ's soft azz hold the strap no more," he said as they shared a laugh together.

"Oh, Fatty Mack and Lil Mickey said they finna stop by too. Fatty want you to see some car he just pulled out and Lil Mickey tryna sell his Lesabre, he gotta turn himself in next week," Jamillah said. Fatty Mack and Lil Mickey were her older cousins. Fatty Mack used to get it out the mud, then he went legit and started buying all type of properties, he owned everything from a clothing store, to a car wash, to a gas station.

Lil Mickey owned properties as well. Up north, he was a big-time heroin dealer who did some pimpin as well, he was eating good.

"Oh yeah, when they comin'?" Richie said, getting up and heading to the closet.

"They should be pulling up soon, they called about an hour ago. And that money is a little over forty-nine thousand," she said before turning to leave. He knew that she had counted it already.

"Aight," Richie said looking through his closet for something to wear. He knew Fatty and Mickey were Jordan fanatics and so was he, so whenever they got together it was battle of who wore it best because they all pretty much had every Jordan in the number system.

Richie decided to go all Jordan as he grabbed his black, red, and white throwback Chicago Bulls #23 jersey and laid it on the bed before putting on a pair of all black Moncler shorts with the matching belt. Putting on his socks, he reached in the closet and grabbed his black and red Air Jordan retro "Infrared" #6's. Any true Jordan sneaker head knew that the holes in the tongue were to symbolize the scoreboard. Tinker Hatfield was always good at designing things within the Air Jordan's he created.

Putting his shoes on, he threw the jersey on, his plain jane Franck Mueller watch, and his icy double R Rolls Royce piece that stood for Richie Rich. Brushing his hair, he then put his black, red, and white Chicago Bulls snapback on backwards. Looking in the mirror, he knew that they better had come correct if they were trying to out due him today.

"Richie!!" Jamillah yelled.

"What up bae!?"

"Fatty said he finna pull up"

"Aight," Richie said, then put his F&N in his waistband. After yesterday, he couldn't afford to leave home without it. After grabbing his phone and keys, he went into the kitchen and grabbed a bottled water before going outside.

Opening the water, Richie took a couple of swigs, then he heard the lyrics, "I pimp down the Ave and I'm lookin' good/diamonds up against that wood." UGK's "Diamonds Up Against That Wood" was blaring from the car bending the corner. It was an all-white 1978 drop Cadillac Coupe Deville with a couple red soft top and all white guts with red piping.

He done got me again, Richie thought to himself when he looked down and saw the 26" chrome spinning Jumpman logo rims. Richie ain't never seen no shit like that before and he had to admit, Fatty Mack snapped.

The 5'10 brown skinned Fatty Mack turned the music down and hopped out the drop running his hands over his waves. He was dressed in white and red Louis Vuitton with white and red low top retro #11 LS Air Jordan's, and an icy 2six piece because he was originally from 26th and Brown. He was smiling hard knowing he was killing the game with his Lac.

"What's good my brother?" he greeted Richie with a handshake.

"Chillin', the drop went stupid crazy. Where the fuck you get those rims from?" Richie asked while looking at them as they had yet to stop spinning.

"I got those custom made for a little of nothing."

"Let me buy 'em," Richie shot already knowing the answer.

"Absolutely not, you know I'mma member of team Jordan," he laughed. But he was serious, he loved his Jordan's. "I see you out here with the retro 6's, huh?" he added.

"Yeah, you know what the tongue is supposed to be?" Richie shot, thinking that he had one.

"Absolutely, the scoreboard," he retorted.

Damn, Richie thought as they laughed until they heard the crisp words to "All Eyez On Me" by 2pac thumping down the block. They turned to see an outrageous sky blue colored 1979 2 door Buick Lesabre on 28" chrome Forgiato rims pull up and park right behind Fatty's drop. Turning his music down, the 6'5 light skinned Lil Mickey hopped out with his corn rows to the back dressed in white and sky-blue Polo attire with the white and Columbia patent leather retro #11 Air Jordan's.

"What's good fellas?" Lil Mickey asked shaking their hands and showing his six on top platinum and diamond teeth.

"Shit chillin' fam," Richie said while looking at his iced-out Palmer and Concordia piece and chain.

"I'm good cuz," Fatty Mack said

"I see everybody out here wit the Jay Bones on," Lil Mickey smiled referring to their Air Jordan's.

"Yeah, and Fatty went crazy with the Jay Bone rims too," Richie said smiling.

"He fucked the city up, didn't he? When I first seen 'em, I wanted 'em too, but I ain't wanna knock cuz idea, because he always gon' be known as the one who did it first."

"I feel you, so you finally selling the Lesabre?" Richie asked, a little surprised.

"It's time for me to let her go, I gotta turn myself in next week. I gotta serve two years for my pistol case When I get out, I'mma flip an Alpha Romeo or something that nobody in the city got. I know you was always asking me if I wanted to sell it, and you fuck with my lil cousin too, so I wanted to give you top priority," Lil Mickey explained.

"That muthafucka wet, who painted it?" Richie asked.

"Javi."

"Puerto Rican Javi who got the shop on South 27th?" Richie inquired.

"Yeah, that's my dude," Lil Mickey said.

"Yeah, Javi cold, he got the city on lock with the paint. He painted my Impala and my truck," Richie said. "What you want for it?" he added.

"For you, gimme twenty-five gees and it's yours," Lil Mickey retorted.

"Umm," Fatty Mack said knowing that was a sweet deal. He knew his cousin put at least twice that amount into that car. "I'm damn near gon' buy it if you don't," he continued.

"I get to keep the rims too?" Richie asked.

"Yep, that muthafucka got a brand new 383 stroker engine in there that I just put in less than a year ago, 400 trans, chrome carburetor, 3 JL Audio subwoofers in the truck, pushed by two Zeus amps, and all white guts. I paid 10 for the paint, and we ain't gon' even get on the rims," Lil Mickey explained. But he didn't have to convince Richie; it was sold as far as he was concerned.

Besides, he was gon' use the money he won yesterday, so it was damn near free.

"Bet, you got the title with you?" Richie asked.

"It's in the glove box."

"I'm finna go in the crib and grab the cash for you right now," Richie said before walking off and taking a swig of his water. Going in the house, he went inside the bedroom, counted out twenty-five thousand, put it in a brown paper bag, and set it aside. Then he counted out 15 gees and stuffed them in his pocket. When he got to the spot, he was going to call his plug Ant, and have him drop him off a half brick. *It was time to turn up even more,* he thought as he grabbed the brown paper bag, and headed outside.

*****

Richie Rich swerved through block after block jackin' hard in his new Lesabre subbing "Bag on me" by A Boogie Wit the Hoodie featuring Don Q. He had Jamillah behind him in his Impala with Fatty Mack and Lil Mickey trailing her in the drop.

Richie was feeling good. Every side street intersection that he stopped at, he would swerve to the opposite side of the street and slap the stop signs as he passed them while still seated in his seat. He was surely sitting high enough to do it.

Pulling up on 39th and Garfield, they made a left turn and pulled up on the left side of the street to see Chauncey and RJ on the porch looking as they came to a stop in front of the spot.

"What's hat-nen boy?" Richie said, hopping out smiling.

"Shit, I see you done copped a new whip," Chauncey said.

"Yeah I did, but I ain't buy it for me."

"Who you buy it for?" Chauncey asked.

"You if you want it my nigga, but I'm keeping those rims," Richie said shaking his hand and one arm hugging him while catching the look RJ had on his face. But Richie didn't give a fuck. Chauncey saved his life, so giving him a car was only a small token for keeping him alive. "My nigga, you was there for me and stood up for me when I needed you most, so I wanted to show you my gratitude," he continued.

"It's love my nigga, you would've did the same thing for me."

"No doubt about it, so you ready to get in traffic?" Richie asked, handing him the keys.

"Hell yeah, let's scoot by my bitch house so I can jack on her bum azz cousins," Chauncey laughed. He couldn't believe his boy had bought him a car.

"Fo sho, but I gotta stop a few places on the way and catch some action."

"Aight," Chauncey said.

"But before we go, you heard anything on ole boy?" Richie asked.

"Word on the street is the nigga in ICU, they say he gon' make it. I hollered at my cousin Kevin and he said dude a major nigga off Keefe Street, so we gotta keep our eyes peeled in case one of his people feeling heroic and try to ride down on us," Chauncey explained.

"You got yo ratchet on you."

"You know the thirty stay with me."

"Okay, just make sure you watching out while we rolling, ain't shit finna stop us from being our here, too much money to be made. Let me give this shit to ole boy, then you follow me," Richie said

"Cool," Chauncey said before making his way to the Lesabre as Richie went on the porch and gave RJ the 15 gees.

"When Ant come through, give him this and put the half of brick up that he gon' give you for me, don't do nothing else, just put it up," he stated firmly before turning to leave.

"Bro, you bought that nigga a car?" he asked in disbelief which completely pissed Richie off as he turned back around.

"Firstly, don't question what the fuck I do with my money. Secondly, you muthafuckin' right I bought him a car. Shit, if it wasn't for him, I probably wouldn't even be here right now, you remember yo azz froze up in that action and almost let a nigga down me. That car wasn't shit compared to my life, so I bought it to show him the love he showed me by not letting me get killed," Richie said and turned to leave while RJ sat there looking dumbfounded. At that moment, a hatred toward Chauncey developed inside of him because Richie treated him like he was his brother, and when it came to RJ, Richie treated him like a little kid and always tried to chastise him in front of everybody and RJ hated that with a passion. He started to tell Richie to make Chauncey sit up here and get his dope since he did everything so right, but he didn't want a confrontation.

One day he was gon' show his brother that he was in fact a man, and a smart one at that. He watched Richie hop in his Impala with Jamillah and pull off three cars deep.

"Fuck Richie," he said out loud to himself.

CHAPTER THREE

(One Year Later)

"Look who just walked in the club Jazzie girl," Peaches said while looking toward the door.

"Who?" Jazzie retorted. But before she could turn around to see, Peaches had already blurted it out.

"Richie Rich and Chauncey," she replied with greed dripping throughout her tone as well as written all over her face. Richie Rich and Chauncey were best friends and had been making a name for themselves in the dope game around the city, so whenever they came in the club, they always got plenty of attention because they were always generous.

"Bitch is you crazy? All dem niggas want is for a bitch to stuff that bullshit up her pussy, they don't give a fuck if you die doin' that punk azz shit or not," Jazzie stated meaning every word. Jazzie was a light skinned woman with long hair, she stood 5'2 and weighed 140 pounds. Although she was petite, her 32C-26-39 coke bottle frame had men grabbing their crotch every time she walked past. She was easily one of the baddest chicks in the building, people would always tell her that she favored the movie star Megan Good.

"So, what you tryna shake yo ass for the rest of yo life? I know I ain't them niggas holdin', and a bitch like me got bills to pay, straight the fuck up," Peaches shot back. Peaches was dark skinned, 5'8, 175 pounds with micro braids, and a 34-31-42 inch frame. Peaches was all about her money and didn't mind going the extra mile to get it.

"This low budget azz how, now she'll fuck for a buck," Jazzie said under her breath.

"Huh?" Peaches said because she didn't hear Jazzie over the loud music.

"I said the last thing that stretched this pussy out was having my son, and that's gonna be the last thing too," Jazzie explained. She didn't repeat what she said because she knew that Peaches would tear off into her ass if she disrespected her. Needless to say, Jazzie's bark was much tougher than her bite.

"Bitch stop lying, I just saw you the other day gettin' in that Lac truck with that nigga Big Bank and I know he stretched that pussy out the way he tossed all that money on yo ass," Peaches said putting her on blast. Jazzie looked at Peaches in a shocked state because she tried to keep her business discreet and didn't think she had been spotted leaving with Big Bank.

"Damn hoe, get you some business and upgrade on the niggas you fuckin' wit," she replied with her finger in Peaches' face. "And stop worrying about who I'm fucking," she added.

"Yeah whatever, I gotta go anyway, time is money and I will never waste neither," Peaches said while adjusting her thong, then she noticed Tim looking in her direction. Tim was the owner of the club which was called P.T. Everybody thought that stood for Play Time, but those who knew better, knew it stood for Pimpin' Tim's which he was formally known as. But after he gracefully bowed out of the (P)ut it (I)n (M)y (P)ocket game, he took some of his profits and opened up one of the hottest strip clubs in Southeastern Wisconsin.

"Girl don't look, but Tim over there hawkin' the fuck outta bitch," Peaches added while cutting her eyes his way. "He think cause he own this club, he can put his foot down on a hoe like he still pimpin' or somethin', with that weak azz slogan he be saying: I pay you to dance, not stand, and if you in here playin', you certainly ain't staying," she continued in a mocking tone.

Jazzie stared at Peaches and then started laughing because she knew that's exactly how he sounded. Then, as if they practiced it a thousand times, they both said in unison, "Lame." Then, they walked off in opposite directions giggling. Jazzie was headed toward the back, but she felt a pair of eyes on her, so she looked over shoulder to see Tim staring her down. She just shook her head and kept it moving.

Peaches mingled with a few customers on her way to the stage, when she was abruptly stopped by somebody calling for Jazzie. After seeing who it was, she quickly made her way over to Jazzie and tapped her on the shoulder before she could make it to the back. When Jazzie turned around, Peaches tilted her head in the direction where Jazzie was being requested.

"They want you," Peaches said, making sure she knew they wanted her.

"Who?" she asked with her face scrunched up.

"Richie Rich and Chauncey," she said, now pointing in their direction. Peaches knew that if she played her cards right that they would not only shower Jazzie with money, but her as well.

Jazzie turned her head to see them anxiously waving her over. Rolling her eyes, she started to walk slowly in their direction because she already knew what they wanted. As she arrived at their table with Peaches hot on her tail, she gave them a slumped over posture to let them know that she was not in the mood for games. "What nigga," she said, already agitated.

Chauncey looked up at her admiring how her body glistened from the baby oil.

He was infatuated with her small but thick frame, her perky breasts, lush ass, and her face that only had a hint of makeup. The countless hours she spent in the gym had her stomach flat as an ironing board, and the two pig tails that she wore only added to her beauty and set her apart from every other girl in the club. *She supa bad,* Chauncey thought to himself while looking her up and down. Then he said, his normal phrase that he always used whenever he came in the club, "Girl look what money will do for ya." Chauncey leaned back holding both of his arms out, but before he could say another word, she abruptly spoke.

"Dude, what the fuck you want?" she said with her hand on her hip. She knew that Chauncey had a thing for her because he stayed persistent in his approach, but she would never fuck with him like that. She knew he was no good and would do some treacherous shit to further himself along in the game. She had witnessed it firsthand, so there was no way she would put herself in a situation to be the lamb that got sacrificed. Him and her could never be.

"You know what I want, I wanna see you bounce that ass so I can throw this cash," he told her while he stroked the peach fuzz on his chin.

"We both know that's not gonna happen. The last time I danced for you, you stuck yo funky azz fingers in my ass, you nasty bastard. I ain't never fuckin' with you like that again," she replied with a stern look on her face. Hearing this, Richie Rich busted out laughing before he spoke.

"Jazz bring yo thick ass over here, I got some business I wanna holla at you about," he said nonchalantly.

"Don't even think about it, this pussy is for tampons, dicks, and dildos, so try that sorry azz game on another bitch, because this bitch here ain't goin'," she said, pointing to herself while rolling her eyes and turning her lip up.

"I ain't on none of that, I promise," Richie Rich said, putting his hand to his chest over his heart as if he was saying swear to god. "I just wanna put something in ya," he added as Chauncey started to laugh.

"I bet you do," she managed to get out over Chauncey's loud chuckle before Richie Rich followed up with.

"It's a dick the size of a brick," he said and started laughing so hard that his eyes started to water.

"Awww, that just tickled you two muthafuckas silly, huh?" she said while putting her finger on the table and leaning forward."You's a stupid muthafucka and one day you gon' realize just how stupid and naïve you are to the game, and I'll be there to laugh at you. Now get this tramp to do yo dirty work," she added, pointing to Peaches as Chauncey shot her a dirty look.

"Do what?" Peaches asked with her face frowned up totally missing the end of the conversation. "What y'all want me to do?" she continued. Jazzie gave her a bitch please stare, then replied, "Something strange for some change, that's what," she said before walking away from the table heading toward the back.

"I'm about bout that money hoe, you can fake it if you want to, but I gotta have mine," Peaches yelled after her. But Jazzie was already out of earshot, so she turned and focused all of her attention on Richie Rich and Chauncey. "So, what's up?" she continued while adjusting her garter belt that was on her upper thigh and filled with money. Chauncey stared at Peaches for a second. She was decent in the face and strapped, although she had booty do, which was hood terminology for her stomach stuck out further than her booty did. But other than that, she was alright. Chauncey looked at her round mound breasts with the big chocolate areolas and nipples, then he looked between her legs and noticed that her pussy must've been hungry the way it swallowed her thong in the front and made her have a serious camel toe going on. That prompted his next move.

"What that do Peaches?" he asked in a lustful tone while pointing in between her legs.

"It do what the money do for it," she replied.

"Let me see you shake somethin' then," he retorted while pulling a large wad of money from his pocket. When Peaches looked down and saw all that money, she turned around, licked her lips, then slapped her ass giving it a life of its own as she started shaking and twerking it so hard that it looked like she was trying to shake her ass off of her body. Some of the other patrons stopped watching the dancers at their tables just to watch her, and that only encouraged her to go even harder. Chauncey leaned back enjoying every minute of the show. He tried to grip her ass, but she was twerking so hard that her cheeks kept jumping out of his hands. Peaches finally slowed down and allowed Chauncey to jiggle and wiggle her butt. She had him just where she wanted him as he stuffed bills after bills down her thong. So to thank him, she made her ass clap like a standing ovation, and she was not using her hands. Chauncey looked over to see if Richie Rich was peeping how the freak did her thang, but he was on his cellphone. Although he couldn't hear the conversation, he could tell by his boy's demeanor that something wasn't right.

"Be yo azz at the spot, I'll be there in 20 minutes," Richie Rich barked before slamming his cellphone down so hard on the table that it knocked over their drinks and bottles.

"What's hat-nen my nigga?" Chauncey asked hesitantly. Richie didn't say a word, he just nodded toward the door confirming Chauncey's suspicions about this being a serious situation. As they both started to get up, Chauncey told Peaches, "Let me see you shake that thang one mo' time for I get outta here."

"You ain't said nothin' nigga," she said while bending over and proceeding to throw that ass while looking back at him saying, "Dis how you like it?" He threw the remaining money in his hand over her ass.

Chauncey then smirked at Richie Rich before he stuck his index finger in Peaches' ass catching her off guard and pissing her completely off. Peaches jumped up and turned around with her fists balled tightly. "Bitch azz nigga what's yo problem," she said through clinched teeth. Chauncey raised his arms up in effort to protect his face in case she tried to swing on him. "Wit yo pussy azz," she continued her verbal assault on him after seeing his reaction to her getting in his face.

"Come on Peaches, fuck dat nigga," another stripper came up and said before helping Peaches pick her money up.

"This ain't over muthafucka," Peaches barked before walking off.

"You a nasty azz nigga, I just want you to know that. Now go wipe yo shitty azz hands off and let's ride, you ain't gon' believe the hoe shit that just happened," Richie Rich said, shaking his head.

"What?" Chauncey asked curiously.

"Go handle that and I'll tell you on the way," Richie responded. Chauncey walked off toward the bathroom and quickly returned with a serious look on his face.

"Let's get outta here," he said. Richie Rich looked at the iced-out Breitling wristwatch on his wrist as they headed toward the exit. In his mind, he knew something wasn't right, but he just didn't know what as of yet. However, he did know that it would be a long night, and he thought he was prepared as they exited P.T.'s joint and into the grimy streets of Milwaukee.

CHAPTER FOUR

*R*ichie Rich finessed through the streets behind the tints of his wine berry colored Mercedes Benz truck that was sitting on chrome 24" Forgiato rims. The four 15-inch L7 subwoofers pumped out "On Me" by Moneybagg Yo as Richie Rich made a right on 39th and Garfield. Pulling up in front of his spot, he seen his brother RJ standing on the porch looking sour by the face like a child that knew he was about to receive an ass whooping.

"What the fuck happened?" Richie Rich said aggressively as soon as he hopped out of the truck and walked up on the porch.

"Bro....They caught me off guard, it wasn't shit I could do. When I came from the back with the work, they put big boy extendos in my face.... what was I 'posed to do?" RJ said with his arms stretched straight out.

"Didn't I tell you not to do no business with that much work without me here?" Richie Rich stated, disregarding RJ's demeanor.

"I know man," he replied while shaking his head.

"Obviously you don't know cause you did the shit anyway," Richie said as Chauncey hopped out of the truck, walked up, and stood next to Richie Rich. RJ really didn't care to much for Chauncey, so when he walked up, RJ mugged him, then kept explaining to his brother.

"We'll get the shit back, it ain't nothin' bro," he reasoned.

"Says the man that don't have a dime invested in my grind," Richie shot back.

"You know who the niggas is who stuck you?" Chauncey asked.

"One of the niggas name was Clyde," RJ replied.

"Clyde," Chauncey said more in shock than disbelief.

"Who the fuck is Clyde?" Richie Rich asked curiously.

"A stick-up kid off the east, a known stick up kid at that, so I don't know how this nigga didn't know that," Chauncey replied. "He run with this nigga named Gunna that be on the east too," he added while thinking. "And come to think about it, remember that bitch...umm.... Bubbles that strip down at P.T.'s spot? That's his bitch," he continued.

"Who bitch?" Richie Rich asked puzzled, things were still not clear to him.

"Gunna bitch."

"What!" Richie said more out of curiosity than anything because the whole situation wasn't sitting right with him.

"Bro, look what these bitch azz niggas did to my face," RJ said. He had a couple of big contusions on his forehead and a gaping split under his eye. Richie Rich looked at his lil brother and just then realized his face had been battered, but the only thing on his mind was his money and he didn't wanna display any signs of weakness because he didn't know who was all responsible for takin' his shit.

"Fuck yo face nigga, I just took a three-brick setback fuckin' wit you," Richie Rich scolded him. "Anyways, let me find out you got yo hands in this shit, yo face ain't gon' be the only thing that's fucked up," he added. RJ became instantly offended by his brother's acquisitions that he had something to do with the robbery.

"How you gon' say some shit like that? We family before anything, so don't ever come at me like that," RJ stated firmly. RJ was two years younger than Richie Rich at the age of 23.

He looked up to his brother and he also loved what the game had to offer. He strived to become his brother's right-hand man, but he never got the love or respect that he desired because Richie Rich simply thought RJ was a fuck up artist.

"You heard what the fuck I said," he spoke in a harsh tone. As far as he was concerned, everybody was a suspect until he found out otherwise. "So, everything still in the wall?" Richie continued while staring at RJ because all the dope and most of the money that was in the wall was all he had to his name.

"Everything still intact," RJ said, then cut his eyes toward Chauncey.

"How you know?" Richie replied. RJ was hoping that Richie would trust his word and leave it at that because he didn't want to discuss any money in front of Chauncey because of the lack of trust. He really didn't have a valid reason not to trust him, it was more out of Chauncey holding the position of being his brother's right-hand man which he always thought should've been his position. RJ wanted to tell him that they would check it later, but he was in no position to bargain after he got stripped for some of his brother's work.

"I counted it yesterday," he spoke softly.

"What you mean you counted it?" That shit already banded up, so why the fuck you countin' my shit?" Richie asked heatedly.

"Naw, I'm sayin'... I..." he said but was abruptly cut off.

"What the fuck you sayin'. It's always somethin' wit you lil nigga," Richie exclaimed. RJ didn't like his Richie was coming at him one bit, but he reasoned with himself that Richie was just distraught about the robbery, so he didn't stress the issue about it at that time, but he would holla at him about it later on.

"I just thought you'd wanna know what you got exactly," he said coyly.

"So, since you all in my muthafuckin' business, tell me how much I got then," Richie stated, already knowing in his head what it was supposed to be.

"You got 275," he retorted while catching the look Chauncey had on his face out of his peripheral.

"275 what?" Richie asked, knowing that couldn't be right as his breathing quickened.

"275 thousand," he replied so low that he might as well not said it at all.

Chauncey just stared in silence as Richie Rich grabbed RJ by the back of the neck and marched him into the house. "Where the fuck my money at lil nigga? You a hunnid gees short," Richie spat while pushing RJ on the couch. "Matter of fact, let's go check this shit out right now," he added.

RJ got off the couch slowly and walked toward the back room with Richie Rich and Chauncey right behind him. When they entered the room, Richie Rich went into the closet and moved the dummy wall that was tightly snuggled to the back of the closet, then he reached inside the hole, pulled out three bundles of money, passed it to RJ, and reached back in only to feel a block of the 275 thousand. Richie took that out and a duffel bag. Unzipping the duffel, he saw the 12 kilos tightly duct taped still in place.

"So that's the hunnid right there you must've overlooked," Richie said, pointing to the money that RJ held in his hands.

"So er'thang good?" Chauncey asked.

"You damn right it is," he replied.

"Now that this situation is straight, we gotta go deal with this other shit," Chauncey said.

"We!" RJ blurted out with his face scrunched up.

"Yeah nigga, we!" Chauncey replied while staring coldly at RJ. "I don't know what yo problem is, but...." he added, but was cut off.

"My problem is that you ain't got shit to do with this, so just stand yo azz over there til bro ask you somethin', then do what you do best and say yes," RJ spat with a mug. He had been accepting enough of Richie Rich's bullshit, but he was not going to accept nothing from Chauncey.

"Fuck you nigga," Chauncey replied.

"Naw nigga, fuck yo'self," RJ said aggressively as Chauncey chuckled at his antics.

"It's crazy how you tryna talk shit to me when you the cause of all this shit, more than bro know," Chauncey said while staring directly into his eyes.

"What the fuck you talkin' bout?" RJ and Richie said in unison.

"Check it out Richie," Chauncey said while turning toward him. "You remember that hoe Jazzie that strip down at Pimpin' Tim's?" he added as Richie tried to jog his memory.

"Ol girl that was just with Peaches earlier, fat ass, bad attitude."

"Yeah, what that bitch gotta do wit anything?" Richie asked puzzled.

"Everything, this nigga been fuckin' the bitch," Chauncey said.

"So, what!" RJ barked.

"You know she put the pussy on this nigga and he ran his mouth about havin' shit like he was the one holding," Chauncey said logically. Richie Rich processed all the information at hand and knew Chauncey's assumption could possibly be accurate, so he then turned toward RJ with a straight face and said, "Is that true bro," in a low tone.

"Man, all I told the bitch was we havin' cock suckin' cash, I ain't never say where it was or how much we got, on er'thang," RJ explained.

"We! Where the fuck you get this we shit from, that's my shit nigga. So why the fuck is you discussing my finances with this bitch like it's yo shit. What the fuck is wrong with you," Richie said through clinched teeth.

"Oh, and I heard that Jazzie and Gunna are cousins," Chauncey said, adding fuel to an already lit fire.

"You bullshitin," Richie retorted before he curiously turned toward Chauncey. "How the fuck you know all this shit?" he continued.

"Er'body and they mama know that shit," he said nonchalantly.

"I get money man, I ain't got time to be worrying about who some kin to a punk azz stripper bitch. What I do know is shit startin' to get clearer to me, and once I put this shit in perspective, I promise somebody's gonna die," Richie spoke as the room fell silent for a couple of minutes. "Call Jamillah and tell her I said it's a wipe down," he added, breaking the silence.

"Do you really gotta do that?" Chauncey asked.

"Nigga don't question how I'm doing my shit over here, I got this. So just call Jamillah and tell her what the fuck I said....Matter of fact, don't do shit, I'mma call her my muthafuckin' self," Richie Rich said then pulled out his iPhone from his pocket and walked toward the door as Jamillah answered the phone. "What's good? ...I'm alright, but I need you to come to the castle, it's a wipe down.... Yeah, I know. RJ and Chauncey gon' be here waiting on you.... Alright....you too, bye," he said and ended the call. "She'll be here in a minute, y'all handle that while I go take care of somethin'," he continued before walking straight out the front door and slamming it as hard as he could.

Chauncey stared at RJ and shook his head. "You somethin' else," he spoke.

"Don't say shit to me," RJ spat heatedly.

"No problem."

"I know it ain't," RJ said, mugging him as he sat on the couch waiting for Jamillah to show up.

CHAPTER FIVE

*D*arkness had fallen and the stars looked over the city as Richie Rich weaved in and out of traffic with his mind racing about the latest events. He turned his volume down to 10 to keep his speakers from bustin' as "Blood on the Money" by Future thumped out of them. When he snapped out of his zone, he was pulling up to P.T.'s. He noticed there were more cars out front than usual, especially for it only being 9pm on a Thursday night. Nevertheless, he hopped out and entered the club.

T-pain and B.O.B's "Up Down" was blasting throughout the place when he made it to the main floor where the majority of the strippers were performing. Richie Rich looked around taking in the scenery first before he moved. He saw two strippers at a table grinding and kissing on each other, a stripper on the stage masturbating with a vibrating dildo, and he even noticed the chick in the back of the club sitting on a man's lap and looked to be performing a lap dance, but if you looked closer you could tell that she was fucking him.

Richie Rich then noticed the new white girl on stage, mainly because she was the only white girl there. *This white bitch thick as fuck,* he thought to himself. She had ivory skin and a bodacious butt that swallowed up the thong she had on. He instantly became mesmerized when she touched her toes and pushed her ass back against the pole making it disappear as the onlookers by the stage threw money on her.

She walked to the end of the stage, turned around and started twerking while squatting up and down. Richie Rich had to admit that she was the baddest white broad that he had seen in a while. She was in the category with Ashley Logan, Amber Rose, CoCo, and Iggy Azalea. The white girl then bent over, made her ass wave to the crowd, and when she turned to the side, she noticed Richie Rich's lustful gaze stood out the most. He wasn't hard to spot because the "Garfield" cartoon cat charm with orange diamonds that he had hanging from the platinum chain around his neck sparkled hard when the light hit it. He had the "Garfield" piece done because he was from 39th and Garfield where he put in blood, sweat, and tears to become the man he was today.

Richie Rich stared at the white girl intrigued by her for a number of reasons as she licked her lips and ran her index finger over her pierced nipples which was followed by her winking at him.

Richie Rich acknowledged her with a head nod to let her know he saw her doing her thang, then he headed to the back where the strippers' locker room was.

As soon as he went past the curtain and made it to the door, he was stopped by Pimpin' Tim himself. Pimpin' Tim was an old-school washed-up pimp with a long perm who used his establishment to remind himself of his glory days when he was surrounded by hoes while making money at the same time.

"You can't go back there playa, the sign says dancers only, ya dig," Pimpin' Tim said as Richie Rich turned around to see him dressed in a grey suit with matching gators, his perm done in Shirley Temple curls, and that one gold tooth that always stayed on shine. Richie Rich looked him up and down as Tim got in between him and the locker room door.

"Nigga if you don't get yo Dru Down lookin' azz out my way," Richie stated.

"Listen here young dawg, this my place of business, and you not bout to come in here like you runnin' somethin' tryna start somethin', ya dig," Tim stated.

"I know this yo place, but right now I'm on some bidness shit, so I'd advise you to get the fuck out my way before I smash yo shit in," he replied coldly. But before Tim could say another word, Peaches opened the door and jumped because she was startled to see somebody standing right there. Without hesitation, Richie Rich reached around Tim, grabbed her by the neck, and pulled her close to him. "Where the fuck Jazzie tramp azz at?" he said while Tim just stood there speechless.

"Nigga...I... I don't know." she managed to get out while trying to wiggle herself loose of his grip.

"Bitch I'mma tell you what's gon' happen, I'mma ram yo muthafuckin' face into this wall every time I gotta ask you where that hoe at," he yelled so close to her face that he was spitting on her.

"Oh, hell naw young dawg, that shit ain't finna fly up in here," Tim yelled while on his way to get security. Richie disregarded what Tim was talking about as he continued to apply pressure to Peaches' neck to the point where it caused her to squint her eyes.

"I don't..." she started to say before he ran her face into the wall... BAM!

"You know now!" he barked.

"No," she started to cry as blood trickled out of her nose.

BAM!... This time she hit the wall so hard that it broke her nose and both of her eyes immediately began to darken. "Where the fuck that scandalous azz bitch at!?" he said outraged, before he slammed her face into the wall three more times before she started to feel like she was becoming unconscious. Her legs began to weaken and caused her to fall. Richie Rich kneeled beside her, grabbed a fist full of her hair in his left hand, and slapped the shit out of her with his right hand to make sure she regained full consciousness. Then, he drew back his fist prepared to knock her out if she didn't answer his question.

"Bitch don't make me have to ask you again," he spoke in a low harsh tone.

"O-Okay...Okay," she said in between coughs. She tried to stay true to Jazzie, but she was in fear that he was going to kill her if she didn't say somethin'. "She left about an hour ago with her cousin," she muffled.

"What cousin!" he yelled while yanking her head back.

"Gunna...Gunna came to pick her up, that's all I know," she said in an angry shrill.

Just as he let her go, Tim came rushing toward the back with two big linebacker looking security guards. He was even more pissed when he seen what Richie Rich did to Peaches.

"What the fuck you do to my hoe, I mean Peaches, get his azz," Tim said, motioning for the guards to grab Richie.

"If anyone of you punk azz niggas put y'all hands on me, they gon' have to roll y'all the fuck up outta here," he said while pulling out his F&N with the 30 round extended clip. Then he stared at both security guards. When they didn't move, he said, "That's what the fuck I thought, extendos turn niggas to hoes, believe that."

"Just leave man, that's all I want. I don't want no problems in here," Tim said.

"I'm finna leave, but I'm comin' back, so tell Jazzie she need to get up with me first before I see her," he said while looking at Peaches who was sitting on the floor leaning up against the wall, crying with her head back trying to stop her nose from running like a bloody faucet.

With gun in hand, Richie Rich backed away from everybody because he was not going to turn his back and let them try to pull some bullshit, so he kept his eyes on them. When he got to the curtain, he pulled it back, tucked his pistol away, and made his way back to the main floor where he spotted Bubbles coming in his direction. She gave him a sly wave and a smile as she continued walking toward him.

"What up Richie Rich?" she smiled. By her reaction, Richie Rich could tell she didn't have a clue as to what was going on with the robbery or either she was a damn good actor.

"Shit, what up wit you?" he glared directly into her eyes trying to find any inconsistency in her demeanor.

"I'm just giving niggas the illusion of what they want but never gon' get, so they keep comin' out them pockets hoping to get in this pocket, ya feel me?" she said, pointing both index fingers in between her legs. Bubbles was a brown skinned, butter faced broad, meaning everything looked good but her face. However, her body was nothing other than remarkable and she knew that, so every time she worked, she pranced around as naked as the day she was born with a garter belt on each thigh and a pair of 4inch Saint Laurant heels. If Richie wasn't there on bidness, he surely would've tried to get in that hot pocket too, the way that thang poked out.

"Yeah, I feel you, but I'm tryna get in contact wit yo nigga, you know where I can find him?" he inquired. Bubbles was surprised by his question because she knew Gunna's line of work, so if Richie was looking for him, she knew it couldn't be good.

"He be on the Tray's, so you can find him there or do you want me to call him?" she replied while looking over her shoulder to see if anybody was signaling her to dance. Needless to say, she was not comfortable having this conversation with Richie.

"Naw," Richie Rich responded, knowing damn well she was lying, but he kept his cool. "I'll catch up wit him another time, and by the way I'm throwing a party tomorrow, so you know I'mma need some entertainment, so you should come through and party wit us. You already know money ain't an issue wit me," he continued knowing she wouldn't be able to resist his offer.

"Yeah, I'm wit that. Can I bring the new white girl wit me, she cool as hell and she a bad bitch, I promise she is," she retorted.

"What's her name?"

"Valerie, but everybody call her white girl Val," she said. Richie Rich knew exactly who she was talking about and after the little demonstration she displayed earlier, he was certainly wit that.

"Yeah, why not," he spoke in a suave tone before telling her to get up with him tomorrow and turning to leave. Richie Rich made it out of the club and was met by a light drizzle of rain, so he quickly jogged to his truck, hopped in, and started it.

"These niggas think it's sweet, but I got somethin' for they azz," Richie said to himself. He knew the code of the streets and he had to LIVE BY IT, but he was ready to DIE BY IT if he had too.

CHAPTER SIX

*R*ichie Rich sat in his living room staring at a large Portrait that hung over his fireplace of his deceased parents. They had been coming home from having dinner one night when some kids fleeing from the police in a stolen car, ran a red light, hit their vehicle t-bone style, and pushed them into the opposite directions traffic were they collided with several cars ultimately causing their fatality. The accident happened two years ago, but it was still so fresh in Richie Rich's mind.

RJ took it hard and so did their younger brother Jacoby, who is now 17 years old and stays with their Auntie across town. Richie Rich hadn't seen Jacoby in a couple of weeks because he and his Aunt didn't see eye to eye with her being a church woman and him being in the streets. After she gave him the rest of his insurance money, she basically told him that she didn't wanna have nothing else to do with him. However, Richie did talk to Jacoby often and always made sure he was straight. Richie Rich's thoughts were interrupted by his cellphone ringing. Seeing Chauncey's number on the screen, he answered it.

"What's good?" he asked nonchalantly.

"Shit, what you on?" Chauncey retorted.

"Tryna piece this shit together."

"I already know, my mind been rambling too. When you coming through?" Chauncey asked.

"I'll be there in a minute."

"Aight, Jamillah came and got that too," Chauncey said matter of factly. Richie Rich already knew that because she called and told him to meet her at the house.

"Aight" he said ending the call then returning to his thoughts. How the fuck they know where the castle was anyway...I understand this nigga RJ ran his mouth to the bitch, but he said he didn't say where the house was...What the fuck made them call him outta all people, it had to be the bitch, or did they just show up?... I can't believe this nigga didn't call me, he don't even know them niggas, or do he? This shit crazy....Richie Rich wrestled back and forth with his thoughts until he heard his phone ring, bringing him back to reality.

"Hello."

"Open the door, I'm pulling up now," Jamillah said.

"Here I come now."

"Hurry up thou because I gotta pee," Jamillah said before ending the call. Richie chuckled before he went to open the back door as she was pulling into the garage. On his way to the garage, Jamillah zoomed past him.

"Hey baby," she said while running into the house. Before he could respond, she was already in the house. Richie got inside the car and did what was required to open the stash box. After a 30 second wait, he heard a loud pop, then he got out of the car, opened the backdoor, raised the seat up, and grabbed both duffel bags. Locking everything back in place, he closed the garage door, and made his way back into the house.

Richie Rich put both bags in the bedroom closet, sat on the bed, and put his face inside his hands. Everything that was happening seemed surreal and he was still trying to wrap his mind around it.

"What's on your mind baby?" Jamillah said, breaking his train of thought while coming into the room. Richie Rich looked up at the woman who kept him grounded and tamed since they were 15 years old and gave her a slight smile. Jamillah was a beautiful dark-complexioned woman who stood 5'5 and 135 pounds, all in the ass and chest areas. Her slanted eyes and long hair always gave an impression that she was mixed with Asian descent.

"It ain't shit that I can't handle," he said, trying to assure her that he was good, but she knew him better than anyone and something was definitely on his mind. "Come on Richie, this me you're talking to. I know you wouldn't have me do a wipe down if something wasn't wrong, this I know, so if you need an ear or a second opinion on something, I am here for you sweetheart," Jamillah exclaimed with sincerity. Richie Rich knew he needed someone to vent to that he could trust for a second opinion if not for anything else, shit, she always provided him with that, so he told her everything that plagued his thoughts.

"I don't know if RJ had anything to do wit it, but I ain't excluding his azz," Richie said, finishing up.

"Listen to what the hell you saying, ain't no way RJ pulled no bullshit like that, you know better than that Richie," she stated.

"Hear me out thou, how the fuck did he get robbed by some Eastside niggas who known for pokin' niggas? First of all, how the fuck they know where that house was when ain't no work gettin' pushed outta there, and secondly, they came to him like he was the man. Why didn't they call me? Ain't no way RJ didn't know what time it was, this the same nigga that was about to let a nigga kill me, I shouldn't be fuckin' wit his azz no way brother or not," he explained. Richie was still pissed about the situation from a year ago. Jamillah processed all the information in her head before she spoke.

"Come on bae, use your head. There's a reason they went to him, you weren't there right?" she asked.

"Nope."

"Okay then, somebody put them on RJ," she said, giving her perspective.

"Yeah, I think it's this bitch named Jazzie that work down at the strip club because that's her cousin," he said.

"Who cousin?"

"Jazzie cousin"

"What?"

"Jazzie cousin is one of the niggas that robbed RJ."

"Oh, what the hell that gotta do with anything?"

"RJ was fucking Jazzie and I think the bitch put her cousin on him because she figured he was having money. Either that or all them muthafuckas in cahoots. All I know is it's a nigga named Clyde, his guy named Gunna whose bitch is Bubbles, and she work at the strip club too."

"How you know all them nasty pole fuckin' bitches anyway? I can't believe you go to places like that anyway, that shit cra..." she said, but was cut off.

"Cut it out, you know ain't shit movin'."

"Yeah whatever nigga, don't get fucked up," she smiled while walking toward him as he grabbed her and pulled her on top of him.

"Ahh!" she screamed trying to get free from him tickling her. Jamillah was the only girl who Richie had ever connected with in a deep intimate way. She fully understood him, and he understood her. Jamillah had been saying her period was late, so at her last doctor's appointment, they found out she was two months pregnant, so they were ecstatic about having their first child together.

"You know I love you, don't you?" he said making her squirm from his cold hands that were creeping up her back to unfasten her bra.

"Yes, and I love you too, but what are you doing?" she smirked.

"You say you love me, so I'mma need some reassurance," he said while dropping her bra on the floor.

"Oh, is that right?" she said while straddling him, pulling her shirt over her head to expose her dark colored areoles and nipples. Richie Rich pulled her close to him kissed her passionately before he latched on to one of her nipples as soft moans escaped her mouth, then he switched to the other nipple. Satisfied with that, he rolled her onto her back, and helped her remove the rest of her clothes.

Richie Rich looked down at her body and licked his lips as she spread her legs apart and made him think it was time for dinner, so he dove in face first and attacked her clitoris with a vicious tongue lashing.

"Ohhh shit" she said while grippin' the back of Richie Rich's head as he stayed on the clit and moved his fingers expertly inside of her. Once he finished with that, he stood to his feet, put his chain on the dresser, stripped down, mounted Jamillah, and slid his fully erect dick inside of her.

"Ahhh," she moaned as Richie thrusted deep inside of her touching her back wall. Jamillah had a super wet shot that

Richie couldn't get enough of, so he threw her legs over his shoulders and long dicked her while she tried running away from it. Switching her into the doggy style position, he slid into her from the back.

"Ohhh Richie!" she screamed as he grabbed a fist full of her hair with one hand, her ass cheek with the other one, and stroked her good. Hearing her moans only excited him as he became animalistic inside of her.

"Arrgghh," he growled as he pounded into her.

"Ohh ohh, get it baby....ummm," she moaned while throwing it back at him making her ass clap against his pelvic area. The two went at it for 45 minutes until he couldn't take it no more and came deep inside of her. Richie Rich pulled out and laid next to her spent while she cuddled up and laid on his chest. After that hell of a sex session, Richie became tired and started to doze off until his phone rung.

"What's good?"

"Dude where you at? Me and RJ still at the castle waitin' on you," Chauncey said.

"I'll be there in twenty minutes."

"Aight luv."

"Luv," Richie Rich said, ending the call. Then he looked down at Jamillah who was asleep on his chest. He moved the hair from in front of her face and kissed her forehead, then slid from under her and made his way to the bathroom to shower.

After that he handled his hygiene, he then dressed in all black True Religion jeans, black tee, black True Religion hoodie, and a pair of all black #3 'Blackcat' Air Jordan's. Every Jordan sneaker head knew the #3's were a staple in the Jordan collection because they were the first Jordan's to have the Jumpman logo.

"You leaving baby?" Jamillah asked while turning over.

"Yeah, I'll be back later on tonight," he said as he pulled his black skull cap on his head.

"You be careful out there and don't accuse nobody of nothin' until you know for sure, because if you make that accusation against someone innocent, friends can ultimately turn into enemies," she spoke sincerely

"You right, I'll see you later on tonight," he said while walking over to kiss her lips and rub their unborn child in her stomach.

"I love you."

"I love you too," he said then stuffed his .40 with the extended clip in his waistband, grabbed his phones, and left the house. Twenty minutes later he pulled up on 39th and Garfield. Hopping out of his truck, he made his way into the house.

"What's good fam?" Chauncey asked.

"Coolin' fool" Richie Rich said as he sat on the couch. "I got a plan and it's going down tomorrow, shit go how I'm expecting it to, I'll have the answer I'm looking for," he continued.

"Yeah...so what is it?" Chauncey asked.

"You'll see tomorrow," he grinned, then pulled out a bag of moonrock kush, tossed it to RJ and said, "Roll dis up." RJ grabbed a CD cover off the speaker, resumed his position on the couch and started breaking the blunt down.

"So, where this plan gon' take place?" RJ asked out of curiosity

"Right here at the castle," he said while accepting the blunt from RJ. Then, he put some flame to it, leaned back, took a deep puff, and slowly exhaled a big cloud of smoke.

"Right here?" Chauncey asked, surprised. "I don't think that's a good idea my nigga," he added.

"Why not? It ain't no secret about the location no more, niggas done already ran up in this bitch, so fuck it," Richie Rich said while he closed his eyes, leaned back, took another puff, and blew the smoke toward the ceiling. Chauncey didn't know what Richie Rich had planned for tomorrow, but he'd be there for him any way he could.

"Whatever you wanna do, I got your back on my daddy I do," Chauncey said as he accepted the offered blunt.

"That's what's hat-nen," Richie Rich said and gave him some dap. RJ didn't say nothing, he just sat there with his eyes closed.

*****

Bubbles pulled the curtain back and walked to the dressing room after finishing up her set. She was startled when she seen Peaches standing off to the side by the locker looking a hot mess.

"Girl, what the fuck happened to you?" she asked as she noticed the big contusions on her forehead and seen her hair was in disarray as she wiped blood from her nose.

"That bitch azz nigga Richie Rich smashed my face into the wall," Peaches replied quickly.

"For what?" Bubbles said. She faked concern, but on the inside she was laughing like a muthafucka at how bad he fucked her up.

"All I know is he asked me about Jazzie and some bullshit about her taking his shit while he kept pounding my face into the fuckin' wall wit his bitch azz." she whimpered trying to flip her hair back into place. "Well, he throwin' a party tomorrow and he invited me and Val to go shake somethin' and get this money," she said while throwing both her hands in the air and twirling her hips around like she was doing the hula hoop. If Bubbles was smart, she would've sensed trouble after Richie Rich was looking for her boyfriend, her friend who whooped her coworker's azz, and wanted her to come to his private party, but she was blinded by greed.

"Bitch if I was you..." Peaches started to say but was cut off.

"And you're definitely not. So, miss me wit that, I gotta do me," Bubbles said, then leaned forward and made her ass wave from side to side. "They can't get enough of this," she added as white girl Val walked in the locker room. "Hey girl, come here once," she continued.

Val made her way over to where Bubbles and Peaches stood with a curious look on her face because she knew Peaches was not a fan of hers, so she had no idea what they were on even though her and Bubbles were cool.

"What's poppin' girl?" Val asked as she walked up standing like a brick house at 5'6, 155 pounds, bow legged, thick hips, a flat stomach, and an astonishing 34DD-25-41-inch frame. She wore a bald head hairstyle with designs cut on one side.

"Shit, I was tryna see if you wanted to go to this party wit me and get it poppin'," Bubbles said.

"What party?"

"The nigga that was in here earlier, tall and dark chocolate with all the ice on. You know who I'm talkin' bout?" she asked.

"With that Garfield cat chain?"

"Yep."

"Mmm, I definitely know who you talkin' about. That nigga fine too, what's his name?" Val asked while biting down on her bottom lip.

"Bitch watch yo mouth with that nigga shit," Peaches spat. She joked about a lot of things, but she refused to stand by and let anybody white used the N-word, her great, great Grandma would turn in her grave. Besides that, Val was getting so much attention because she was white with a sistah's body and Peaches didn't like how she flaunted herself.

"Alright, my fault Ms. Farakkan," Val said in a condescending manner while rolling her eyes. She didn't say the N-word to be disrespectful. She grew up around nothing but black people and felt more accepted by them than her own race, so in a way she felt like Peaches was overreacting, but then again, she felt her.

"Richie Rich, the NIGGA name is Richie Rich," Bubbles said putting emphasis on the N-word more toward Peaches. "Anyways, he asked about you and invited us to his party to throw down, so bring yo thong," she added.

"BUT IT WON'T BE ON FO' LONG," they both said in unison and giggled as they turned and made their way to the stage to do a double strip tease set. Peaches just stood there looking crazy while shaking her head. "Hoez," she said under her breath.

CHAPTER SEVEN

*A*s the sun turned into the moon, Richie Rich had everything situated and ready to go as he pulled up in front of the castle and parked behind Chauncey's midnight blue Cadillac CTS that was parked behind RJ's orange and yellow '85 Cutlass Supreme

Richie Rich looked and noticed that the porch light was on which was their signal for everything was good in the house, then he blew the horn once and stepped out into the 2017 mid-March cool breeze and put his hood on his head.

Making his way into the house, he immediately started making a few last-minute adjustments. As Richie placed a chair directly in the middle of the floor,

RJ and Chauncey walked into the living room from the kitchen.

"What's goin' on?" he said, greeting them both.

"What's good fam," Chauncey replied before he finished rolling his blunt as he sat on the couch.

"So, what's the plan bro?" RJ said leaning against the wall.

"You'll see in a minute," Richie Rich smiled while accepting the offered blunt. As soon as he exhaled, the doorbell rang. "Right on time," he added as Chauncey went to get the door. Chauncey overheard a lot of giggling as he got closer to the door, then he looked through the peep hole.

"It's them bitches from the club," he said.

"Let 'em in then," Richie Rich said. Then, the door swung open and there stood Bubbles and white girl Valerie together looking like a chocolate and vanilla swirl ice cream cone on a hot summer day.

"Come on in ladies," Chauncey said, then gestured, stepped to the side, and allowed them to enter. As they walked in, Chauncey got a whiff of their intoxicating fragrances and immediately hoped they were gonna sell some pussy because he was surely gonna buy some.

"What up Richie Rich?" Bubbles said, walking into the living room. "Look who I brought wit me," she added while turning toward Val. Richie Rich stared expressionlessly, then he smirked and nodded in her direction. She was even badder than what he initially thought up close.

Val waved and smiled with a shy innocent look on her face as she walked over to the couch to put her jacket and purse down, when outta nowhere, Bubbles grabbed her by the arm and pulled her into the middle of the floor by the chair and said, "Girl let's show these niggas what we bout." She didn't have to tell Val twice as she slowly started jiggling her ass while rotating her hips in a circular motion, catching the attention of everyone in the room.

When she peeped the look on Richie Rich's face, she took it a step further and made her ass clap in the pair of sky blue leggings that she wore which fit like a second skin, then she made it sway from side to side. Richie Rich swallowed the lump in his throat as Chauncey and RJ got closer to the action.

Val took her tank top off revealing a white bra, then she leaned forward slowly with her ass facing Richie Rich and peeled her skin tight pants from her body until she was only in her bra and a white see through thong that was so little, it looked as if it could've been a piece of ass floss rather than some underwear.

Val looked over her shoulder to see Richie Rich adjusting in his seat while smoking his blunt trying to look all nonchalant, but she knew he was turned on by what he was seeing, so she turnt up even more. When she faced him, she pulled her thong up into her pussy until the lips popped out of both sides, then in one swift movement, she turned and put one leg over the chair like she was mounting a horse as Bubbles hit play on the radio. Waka Flocka Flame & Drake's "Round of Applause" blared out of the speakers as she bent over and gave a round of applause by making her ass clap before she threw her head back and got to grindin' in the chair like she was riding a dick. She did all of this while staring directly at Richie Rich who just stared with a half-smile, half-smirk on his face.

Val got off the chair and positioned herself in the doggystyle position with her legs wide opened and put her face into the floor.

RJ went over to get a look at her from the back as she shook her ass. He could see her pussy swallowing her thong with every thrust, which made him dig into his pocket and make it rain all over her. Richie Rich even got lost in a trance after seeing all that pokin' from the back. *Damn, look at the monkey on that honky,* he thought to himself.

Bubbles felt left out when she seen Val getting showered in all that cash, so she stripped down and started doing what she was known for: twerking.

Getting down on her knees, she bent over, and got to throwin' that ass. Needless to say, she was gettin' it in.

Bubbles then flipped up into a headstand and got to twerking upside down, then she spread her legs straight out into a split before flipping down and making each ass cheek bounce individually. Seeing this, RJ and Chauncey jumped from Val and gotta throwing money on Bubbles which only made her go bananas.

Bubbles laid on her back, moved her thong to the side, then she spread her lower lips apart displaying its pink interior. Then she rolled onto her stomach, got back on all fours, and made her ass clap as Chauncey stuffed $20 bills in her thong.

When nobody was looking, Chauncey slid his thumb in his mouth and moistened it with his saliva, and when Bubbles pushed back while she twerked, Chauncey pushed his thumb up her ass.

Bubbles rolled over and hopped up with the quickness of a housecat. "What the fuck is wrong wit you muthafucka, don't you ever put yo punk azz fingers in my a..." But before she could say another word, Richie Rich stepped in and slapped her so hard that she crashed to the floor.

"Where the fuck yo nigga at bitch!?" he growled while standing over her with his fists clinched. Everybody in the room stared in shock, and the only thing that could be heard was the music. Val stepped backwards until her back was against the wall as she stared with a nervous look on her face.

"Turn that muthafuckin' music off!" Richie Rich shouted, and without hesitation Chauncey went and turned it off. "I said where yo niggq at? And I ain't gon' ask you again," he added as he bent down and grabbed a fist full of her hair.

"How the fuck I 'posed to know?" she replied with her hands up as a defense mechanism. "Dat nigga stay in the streets. He only call me when he wants some pussy," she added as Richie Rich raised his hand to slap her again, but she spoke up quickly.

"Don't hit me no more. I'll call the nigga, it ain't even that serious."

"Call him then bitch," he said standing to his feet and tossing her his cellphone. Then, he turned toward Val and said, "Sit yo azz down." She immediately did, but in a strange way his aggression was turning her on and that was evident by her response.

"Yes daddy."

"Richie Rich caught her response, but he brushed it off because he was strictly on bidness at that point. However, he would keep that in mind for a later time.

"He ain't answering."

"You betta call him back or I'mma give you what he gon' get," Richie Rich barked. "Y'all take my shit and think y'all gon' get away wit it, y'all got me fucked up," he added.

"What the fuck is you talkin' about?" Bubbles asked, oblivious to the situation.

"Bitch shut the fuck up and call him," he shot back.

RJ walked over, looked out the window, and scanned the block to see if anyone heard the ruckus that was going on. Chauncey just stared down at Bubbles with a look of regret and pity.

"Gunna! Where the fuck you at?" Bubbles yelled through the phone as she started crying. "This nigga over here puttin' his hands on me talkin' bout you got his sh..." she added but was cut off by Richie Rich snatching the phone from her.

"I think you got somethin' that belongs to me, nigga," Richie Rich said calmly as Gunna started laughing.

"First off, who the fuck you think you is callin' my line like you bout that life. Secondly, I ain't got shit that belongs to you, this my shit hoe azz nigga," Gunna responded. Richie Rich heard a male and female voice in the background who he assumed to be Jazzie and Clyde.

"Okay tough guy, check this out, I'mma beat the shit outta yo bitch, then I'mma send you a body part every day until I get my shit back. Think it's a game if you want to pussy," Richie Rich spat, then he looked at the phone and thought, *Is this nigga serious?* after hearing him hysterically laughing.

"You's a clown azz nigga just like I thought..." Gunna said before the line went silent because Clyde was whispering something to him.

"Hello," Richie Rich said.

"Meet me at the gas station on Humboldt and North in an hour. And as far as the bitch goes, you can beat her, fuck her, kill her, or whatever you want, I don't give a no fuck. I ain't no tender dick azz nigga, I don't give a fuck about the bitch," Gunna said as laughter could be heard coming from the background.

"Bring Clyde and Jazzie wit you," Richie Rich said. He was tired of all these punk azz games.

"One hour hoe nigga," Gunna said before the line went dead.

"What he say?" Chauncey asked.

"Yeah bro, what his bitch azz say?" RJ asked just as curious as Chauncey. Richie Rich paused, looked down at Bubbles, then shrugged his shoulders, and calmly said, "He said fuck this bitch."

"What!" Bubbles belted out in disbelief. After the conversation, Richie Rich wanted to leave her azz stankin' behind a dumpster, but too many people knew she was with him including Gunna and Clyde. So if she came up missing, he didn't know if they would keep it in the streets or turn state, and he wasn't about to gamble with that, so he took the lesser approach for right now. Walking over to Bubbles, he said "Blame yo nigga fa' this." Then, he swung and knocked her azz out.

"What's the plan now my nigga?" Chauncey asked hopping to his feet.

"We gon' meet these niggas in a hour, but we gotta get this bitch up outta here for now. We ain't letting her go until we get the shit back." Richie said. "RJ," he added as he walked over.

"What's good bro?"

"Take these keys and take that bitch to the old Lena's on Fond du Lac behind the Milwaukee mall. Take her through the back door and into the basement. I just bought the property so ain't gon' be nobody there. Tie her azz to a chair and call one of the little homies to watch her. Can you handle that?" Richie Rich asked.

"Yeah, I got you bro"

"Because I'mma need you wit me on this," Richie said sternly. "Now get the bitch, call lil homie, and call me as soon as you're done so I can tell you where to meet us at and tell them lil niggas not to let her outta their sight," Richie Rich continued. "You staying," he added, talking to Val as RJ bent down and grabbed Bubbles by the arm and helped her as she staggered to her feet.

"Come on got dammit" he told her while putting her arm around his neck.

"I'mma call you as soon as I get everything in order bro," RJ added.

"Aight," Richie Rich said, hoping that he didn't fuck this up. "We got an hour before we 'posed to meet them, so keep that in mind," he added before they left out of the door.

"You think that nigga gon' be able to handle that shit?" Chauncey asked.

"He betta, shit he the reason we going through this, so he gotta make it right."

"You right, I'm finna step outside for a minute and let you holla at 'ol girl," Chauncey said before walking to the door.

"Stay on point, I don't know if them niggas gon' ride through or not," Richie told him. Chauncey knew that was possible, so he checked the 9mm glock in his waistband and made sure he had one up top before he left out of the door.

Richie Rich turned his attention to Val who was now sitting on the couch. She stared back at him with a curious look on her face wondering what was going to happen next, and why he told her to stay.

Richie made his way over to the couch, sat next to her, pulled out a half ounce of that moon rock kush, and rolled up a blunt without saying a word, so Val sat quietly until he broke the silence.

"I might need you to do something for me down the line, you down wit that?" he asked while using the lighter to dry the blunt, setting flame to it, and taking a few puffs before passing it to Val.

"I'm down for almost anything if I'm getting paid," she said before taking a long pull of the blunt. But the potent weed was too much for her lungs and caused her to start coughing hard.

"Let me get that from you lil mama, you can't be hittin' no kush like that, this the best thang smokin'," he said. He laughed at her when he noticed that her eyes turned blood shot red, then he continued the conversation. "I see the fire in your eyes and the determination to make it where you tryna go, so I wouldn't ask you to do nothing for free. I know how the game goes. Now, I respect yo hustle down at the club, but if you really tryna get it, you need to fuck wit me, and I'll help you, feel me?" Richie Rich said, knowing she could come in handy with moving the work amongst several other things.

"I feel you as long as that money stacking up," Val replied with a smile.

"Is money the only thing that motivates you?"

"Money make the world go round. Those who have it want more, and those who don't have it do everything in their power to try and get it. So, you can say that it motivates me in a sense, but I'm not thirsty for it, there's a difference," she replied in her sexiest voice while reaching for the blunt to have another go at it. Richie Rich nodded his head in agreement, he liked the way she thought.

"I'mma trust you to keep what we talked about as well as what you seen here today between us because loyalty is everything to me and I hope you fully understand that," he said firmly while staring at her. Sometimes the simplest of conversations come across in a big way. Val read in between the lines and knew exactly what he was saying. She was about to speak until Chauncey came back into the house.

"Let's get this shit on the road my nigga." Chauncey stated.

"Aight, we gon' drop her off on the way."

"No doubt," Chauncey said while getting the Draco with the 50-round clip from the closet and putting one up top. He was determined to show that he had what it took to get down on something.

*****

"What chall gon' do to that fool?" Jazzie asked after realizing that she had just involved herself deeper than she initially planned.

"What you mean what we gon' do? We gon' strip his azz for everything and if he get outta line, we have his pussy azz lookin' at the ceiling of the church," Clyde replied.

"That nigga bet not say shit stupid, you should've heard how he tried to turn up on me over the phone knowing this ain't what he want," Gunna said, still pissed off about the phone call. "If he called you, then he probably knows the link between me and his brother," Jazzie stated worriedly

"Don't lean on it lil cuz, he ain't that bright. Bro want all that shit, so I'mma handle everything," Gunna told her confidently

"I sure hope so, my son stay here too and I'm not putting him in harm's way for no muthafucka," she said, starting to feel like shit was coming back to bite her already. She liked RJ but taking care of her son was her number one priority.

"We good, just be cool," Gunna reassured her that everything was under control.

"What about Bubbles, y'all just said fuck her, huh?" Jazzie said.

"She in good hands, like All State," Gunna laughed.

"Okay, I sure hope so," she said concerned.

"Enough of this shit, let's get in traffic fam and go handle this business," Clyde said as his phone rang. "What up fool?" he answered, then listened to what was being said. "Oh yeah, alright. I'mma handle that...text it to me...Aight love," he added as he ended the call."Gunna, get Shoddy Mack, Shay, and Rentez on the line. I got a business proposition for my east side niggas," he continued.

"Aight," Gunna said pulling out his phone as they left the house.

CHAPTER EIGHT

fter dropping Val off at the strip club, Richie Rich and Chauncey made their way to the gas station on Humboldt and North Avenue in Richie Rich's black on black tinted up Alero that was used to trap in.

They arrived 15 minutes early, so they could be incognito, knowing Clyde or Gunna wouldn't know what they were driving. About ten minutes later, a gray van pulled up and parked across the street from the gas station.

"Where dem fuck niggas at?" Gunna said impatiently. He and Clyde weren't aware of Chauncey creeping through the alley and quickly approaching their vehicle from a blind spot. "I'm finna call this nigga," he added while grabbing his cellphone. But before he could dial, Chauncey stepped to the window.

"Where that shit at nigga?" he barked with his finger on the trigger of the 50 shot Draco that was aimed at the window, but low enough for the cars passing not to see. Gunna and Clyde both looked to the passenger window and knew exactly who Chauncey was since he was Richie Rich's best friend. "Get the fuck out the car," Chauncey continued as Clyde's phone rang. Clyde held the phone up and said, "Tell yo nigga somebody's on the phone for him, I know he got his coward azz around here somewhere."

"What! I ain't playin,' wit chu niggas," Chauncey spat while taking a step back ready to let the Draco talk for him.

"I ain't playin' wit chu either. If he want his shit back, tell him to come get the phone," Clyde replied. Chauncey stood there with a mug on his face weighing his options. "Now nigga," Clyde added.

Chauncey's index finger stiffened up and he was ready to finger fuck his weapon, but he didn't want to make an irrational decision that would jeopardize Richie Rich getting his shit back. So, he slowly walked backwards away from their car and made his way back to where Richie Rich was parked. When Richie Rich noticed him coming back, he stepped out of the car to meet him.

"Where the nigga RJ at?" Chauncey asked.

"I don't know. I been callin' his phone and it's going right to voicemail," Richie Rich said with a million things racing through his mind.

"That's mighty strange that he ain't here with us when he know what's up. You think that nigga got something to do with this shit?" Chauncey asked.

"Sadly, I was thinking the same shit," Richie Rich said. He couldn't believe that RJ would betray him to this extent, they were blood brothers. "What they on?" he added, trying to stay focused on the task ahead of him even though his mind was fucked up.

"They wanna holla at you."

"For what?"

"I don't know. One of the niggas held they phone up talkin' bout somebody wanna talk to you about gettin' yo shit back. I was gon' air they azz out, but..." Chauncey said but was cut off.

"Naw, not right now,b ut once we get the shit back, we on they azz."

"I know, that's why I didn't."

Richie Rich looked over to the van and saw somebody getting out. He never seen Clyde or Gunna before, so he didn't know who the dude was. So, he pulled out his .40, threw up his arms, and yelled. "What up?"

Clyde returned the gesture, but he held up his glowing cellphone and yelled out.

"Somebody wanna talk to you, they say it's important."

"Say man! Where my shit at, I ain't got time for these pussy azz games," Richie Rich scolded him.

"I think you need to take this call, killa," Clyde responded sarcastically as Gunna got out of the van.

Richie Rich was puzzled as to who could be on that phone. He knew that it betta not been one person though: his brother, RJ. Richie Rich looked toward Chauncey and he had a "you want me to start dumpin" look on his face, but Richie Rich's slight head movement let him know it was a no-go.

Richie Rich's mind was going a thousand miles per minute as he stood there for a moment trying to come up with an instant game plan because things weren't going the way he expected. After a brief debate with himself, he decided to go see who was on that phone for him. As he walked toward Clyde and Gunna with Chauncey following close behind with his trigger finger ready to engage with the slightest inclination of foul play.

When they finally made it over there and stood face to face with the niggas who took his shit, Richie Rich knew he had to show some restraint if he wanted to get his work back, but he had to admit that one of the dudes looked familiar to him.

"So, we finally meet again," Clyde blurted out with a smile as soon as they stopped.

"Where my shit at?" Richie Rich said, wondering what he meant by, "Finally we meet again," because he was unsure if he knew the dude or not.

"Slow down partna, I got yo shit," Clyde said while maintaining the smile on his face. "I can't believe a big baller like yo'self sweatin' me over these crumbs," he added.

"Crumbs! Broke azz bum azz nigga you out here lookin' like you starvin'. I ain't bout to let no nigga take shit from me, I don't give a fuck how much it is," Richie Rich said while gritting his teeth.

"Really," Clyde smiled. "Well I've come to the conclusion that I need more and guess who's gon' give it to me?" he added.

"Who?" Richie Rich replied puzzled.

"You," he responded while tossing him the cellphone.

Richie Rich gripped his pistol tighter. Neither him nor Clyde broke eye contact as Richie put the phone to his ear not knowing what to expect.

"Hello?"

Nothing could've prepared him for what he heard on the other end of the phone as regret quickly set in. The pain was written all over his face as he mumbled out "Jamillah" in a low devastating voice.

"Hearing this, Chauncey pointed the Draco back and forth from Clyde to Gunna which pissed Clyde off as he stared at Chauncey and said, "Shoot," while shrugging his shoulders. When he hesitated, Clyde said, "That's what the fuck I thought, now put that shit up before I get mad."

"What the fuck y'all want," Richie Rich said regretfully after hearing Jamillah's distressed voice. See, Richie Rich was about that drama with anybody until they proved that they would go all out and then he would tuck his tail and let it be.

He didn't think the robbers would come down this hard on him, and now he was feeling like he should've just left it alone and let them take the three bricks that they took. However, it was a little too late, considering that he was already standing in front of them.

"We want the rest of the work and money you got at yo bitch's house," Clyde said as he took Richie Rich's gun from his hand while Gunna took the Draco from Chauncey.

Richie Rich was taken back by the last statement and that was evident by the expression on his face. Clyde noticed the look and spoke on it, "Yeah nigga I know everything."

Richie Rich shook his head in disbelief. *How could you do this to me RJ,* he thought to himself sorrowfully. But for now, he had to get to Jamillah and make sure she was good. "I'mma give y'all everything, but if y'all harm a hair on my baby's head, I ain't givin' y'all shit," he huffed and puffed. "Just follow me," he continued.

"It ain't never that sweet nigga, first let me get them phones," Clyde said as Richie and Chauncey hesitantly handed him their phones. "Now, my boy here gon' ride wit y'all just in case y'all decide to get on some dumb shit. We goin' to yo house," he added while looking at Richie. Richie Rich was starting to wonder why they wanted to take him to his house because he was positive that they had the money already since they pulled a home invasion at his crib and held Jamillah hostage. His thoughts were interrupted by Gunna's words.

"Let's move niggas, we ain't bout to make this an all-night thing."

As they made it to the car, before Richie Rich got in, he gave Chauncey a this shit just got real look. Chauncey nodded knowingly as he slid in the passenger seat and Gunna got in the back with Chauncey's Draco on his lap.

When Clyde pulled his van behind them, Richie Rich started the car, prepared to do what he had to do to protect Jamillah and their unborn child. But for the life of him, he couldn't understand why RJ would do something like this to him. Sure Richie Rich was hard on him, but he never seen it coming back on him like this. Dropping the gear shift into drive, he pulled into traffic not knowing what the night had in store.

*****

As Richie Rich drove, he was trying to figure out exactly what was going on because at the start of the day, he thought he had everything under control, but things were slipping drastically as he pulled up in front of the house that he shared with Jamillah. His eyes shot to the rearview mirror to see Gunna turning around watching Clyde pull up behind them. Richie Rich's stomach started to turn as he was thinking that going inside the house might be a bad idea. But, the love he had for Jamillah clouded his better judgement, knowing he didn't want anything to happen to her because of him.

"Y'all get out," Gunna ordered as he opened his door. When they all got out, Clyde came over to talk to Gunna.

"Rich, the nigga RJ gotta be in there. Why the fuck he doin' all this?" Chauncey asked, seeming like he was paranoid.

"I don't know," Richie Rich said, then shrugged his shoulders wondering the same thing.

"Sorry to keep y'all waiting. Now let's go get that money," Clyde said as he rubbed his hands together.

CHAPTER NINE

*W*hen they entered the house, all that could be heard were cries and sniffling from a woman. Then, they heard a man yell, "Shut up!"

"Jamillah! Jamillah!" Richie Rich yelled as he made his way to the living room.

What he saw crushed his soul to the core. There, in the middle of the floor, Jamillah sat butt naked tied to a chair, bleeding from the mouth, and with a gash on the corner of her eye that could have only come from getting slapped with a pistol. Richie Rich was infuriated as he looked around the room and saw Jazzie and Bubbles from the strip club. *I knew I should've smoked that punk azz bitch,* he thought to himself while looking at Bubbles as she stared back at him with a devious smirk on her face. But RJ was supposed to have Bubbles tied up in the basement of the old Lena's. *I can't believe you did me like this bro,* he thought to himself. He knew that if he made it out of this situation alive, he was going to kill everybody responsible for this situation.

Jazzie was standing off to the side trying her best to look tough, but every time he tried to make eye contact with her, she would turn her head and either look at Clyde or Gunna.

Richie Rich attempted to get over to Jamillah, but Clyde pushed him on the couch.

"Sit yo punk azz down, that bitch aight," Clyde barked.

"So, this how y'all gon' play it," Richie Rich said damn near on the brink of tears realizing this shit was getting deeper by the minute. Then, he looked to Chauncey who just stood there.

"You damn right, look what you did to my bitch face," Gunna replied. Richie Rich looked at Bubbles and seen his handprint still on the side of her face from him slapping her so hard along with her eye darkening.

"Say man..." Richie Rich started but was cut off.

"Say man shit, I don't wanna hear no muthafuckin' pleas," Gunna scolded.

"Where the shit at?" the man that stood next to Jamillah asked.

"Who the fuck is you?" Richie spat to the short dark-skinned man with the waves and face tats. "And where the fuck my brother at? I know he here," he continued. As far as he was concerned, he was through with the games. He wanted RJ to come out and face him like a man.

"Don't worry about who the fuck I am. Now, I asked you where the shit was and if you don't tell me I'mma pop his lil bitch azz," the man said. Initially, Richie Rich thought he was talking about Jamillah, but when he looked, he damn near had to take a double look because the man was pointing his gun at RJ who sat against the wall tied up.

"What the fuck!?" Richie said out loud because shit was not adding up at all. "RJ, I thought you was behind this shit the whole time," Richie Rich stated sadly.

"I'd never do no shit like that to you bro," RJ said firmly as Clyde laughed at them.

"You niggas emotional as a bitch," he said.

"If not you, then who bro?" Richie Rich asked, disregarding Clyde's last comment. But before RJ could respond, Clyde hit him in the face with the gun so hard that his head snapped back into the wall. Richie Rich hopped up in sheer anger but was met by the Draco that Gunna held.

"Sit that azz back down fuck boy," Gunna said.

"I came here to give y'all the shit. All that extra shit y'all doin' ain't caused for," Richie Rich explained.

"This soft azz nigga scared," Gunna said as everybody laughed. Then, he got back down to business. "You came here to give us the shit, so where is it?" he added after turning toward Richie Rich.

"When I give y'all the shit, we done, right?" Richie said, immediately pissing Gunna off.

"I'm tired of you asking all these muthafuckin' questions." 'SLAP' "Just gimme the shit right now," Gunna said after backhanding Richie Rich.

"Richhiieee!" Jamillah shouted before the dude standing next to her slapped her on the side of the head.

"Shut up bitch," he barked.

"Nigga if you put yo hands on her again, I'mma..." Richie started but was cut off.

"You gon' what?" Gunna said, aiming the gun at his head. When Richie didn't say anything, he said, "That's what the fuck I thought, I should blow ya top off," he added pushing Richie Rich's head with the gun. "But since you think this shit a game, I'mma show you it ain't," he continued before looking at Jazzie and Bubbles and giving them a head nod. Jazzie walked over spread Jamillah's legs while Bubbles reached over and grabbed one of the champagne bottles that was lined up over the bar, walked over, and began ramming it inside of

Jamillah's vagina with force causing Jamillah to let out a painful shrill.

The dude that stood next to her, spotted a pair of socks and stuffed them in Jamillah's mouth to muffle her high-pitched screams.

Richie Rich tried to get up to help her, but was hit in the head with the butt of the gun Gunna held. Chauncey stood there with his hands up looking shook as Jamillah continued to squeal in agony and pain as Richie Rich watched on feeling responsible because he was unable to do anything.

"I'm sorry baby, I'm so sorry," Richie sobbed in a regretful tone.

Jazzie and Bubbles stopped momentarily as Jamillah moaned out in sheer pain. She had blood running from her vagina and tears pouring from her eyes. RJ was tied up with his back still against the wall, frustrated and livid as hell that he couldn't do a damn thing about it. Chauncey still stood there with his hands up.

"I'm gon' ask you one more time, where is the dope?" Gunna asked coyly.

Richie Rich realized he made a terrible mistake involving his childhood love in this mess, and everything taking place led him to believe that if he gave up all his work and money, the robbers would kill him because too much damage was done and he had over 300 thousand dollars and 12 kilos. Nobody in their right mind would leave somebody alive to hunt them down for their shit. Knowing this, Richie Rich tried to retract his story in an attempt to not only save his life, but RJ, Jamillah, and Chauncey's as well.

"It's not here, it's at my other house," he said unconvincingly.

"Oh it's here ,this bitch already told me," the dude standing next to Jamillah said while pushing the barrel of the gun against her head.

"No I....." she tried to muffle but was abruptly stopped by dude slapping her across the face with the gun.

"You bitch azz nigga," Richie Rich growled in anger.

"You a hoe, dawg!" RJ yelled, trying to get to his feet.

"Shut yo coward azz up," Clyde said and kicked RJ in the mouth causing his head to hit the wall for the second time.

"Well, all this excitement make a bitch gotta pee," Bubbles said, jumping on Jamillah's lap, pulling her leggings down, and squatting over her face ready to drench her with a golden shower.

"Bitch if you piss on that bitch and leave yo DNA, you leave me no choice but to kill yo azz," Gunna said seriously while pointing his gun at her head.

"I wasn't really about to do that, I was just playin'," Bubbles said while getting off of Jamillah's lap with a look of worry on her face. She was just trying to humiliate Richie Rich for putting his hands on her.

"That's more like it," Gunna said lowering his gun.

"You's a nasty azz trifflin' punk azz bitch," Richie Rich said with disgust.

"Don't say shit to her pussy," Gunner said and punched Richie Rich in the jaw so hard that he rolled off the couch.

"We gon' have to turn it up some because this nigga ain't budgin'," Clyde said to the dude standing next to Jamillah.

"Oh, he gon' come to his senses. Jazzie, Bubbles, fuck that bitch up." Gunna said. And on cue, the two walked over to

Jamillah and Bubbles slapped her around a few times. Then, she grabbed the champagne bottle while Jazzie opened Jamillah's legs. Jamillah couldn't bear to experience the excruciating pain again, so before they violated her once again, she made some noise.

"What you gotta say?" the dude that stood next to her said after he removed the socks from her mouth.

"It's in the back-room's closet, don't put that shit in me no more!" Jamillah said, petrified as she started wailing.

"That's what I thought silly hoe," Bubbles laughed. Richie Rich closed his eyes and shook his head knowing his options had drastically dropped after Jamillah told them where the stuff was, but he also understood why she did it.

Richie Rich felt like time was running out. He was trying to think of a clever move to spare him some time, and just when he thought he had things figured out, he was thrown for another loop.

"Throw me a banger Schod," a voice came from the man that stood next to Jamillah. When Richie Rich looked, he had .357 in his face.

CHAPTER TEN

"Bitch...azz...nigga!" RJ screamed, outraged.

"I can't... What the..." Richie Rich struggled to find the words to say. Then, he found them. "I trusted you with my muthafuckin' life and this how you gon' repay me," he added.

"Fuckin' right, you gotta admit that I played yo azz good," he chuckled. "You think I'm just gon' sit back and watch you get rich while you bird feed me? You got me fucked up. It's because of me you doin' so good now," Chauncey added. "Matter of fact, fuck you 'ol square azz nigga, I don't owe you no explanation, this part of the game," he continued.

"How the fuck you gon' say you the reason I'm doin' so good. I brought yo bum azz in, tried to show you the game, but you spendin' money recklessly trickin' on hoes and shit. Nigga it ain't my fault yo bum azz don't know how to get money. I bought you a twenty-thousand-dollar car and that Cadillac you driving now. What the fuck you want me to do?" Richie Rich said, mugging the shit outta Chauncey. The tension in the room was so thick that you could cut it with a knife.

"I could give a fuck about how you lookin'. Now that I got yo shit, we gon' see how much of a hustler I can become," Chauncey laughed. "I been planning this for a while, but I had to make it look like it was yo lil brother. Once I heard you tell RJ to take Bubbles to the old Lena's, I had to alter my plans. Remember, I told you that I was gon' step outside and let you holla at 'ol girl? That was just the diversion I needed to call my boy Schod and have him intercept that plan, so when you called RJ he wouldn't be able to answer, making him look more guilty while I made you think it was him the whole time. Now that was genius on my part if I may say," Chauncey added.

"You ungrateful bitch, my brother gave you everything short of his blood," RJ stated.

"Man, fuck you and yo brother. I should've let Cash kill his bitch azz that day in the alley. Shit, you was about too," Chauncey replied with a chuckle. Say cuz, grab that work so we can get the fuck up outta here," Chauncey told Clyde. He was ready to get outta there.

"Cuz? Now he yo cousin, huh?" Richie Rich said.

"Actually yeah, he my second cousin. If you would've been using that big azz head of yours, you would've remembered when we got outta Lincoln Hills Detention Center, I took you to all the parties on the East side. I knew you wouldn't remember cuz because he got big azz hell and you dumb azz hell. I'll give RJ credit, he sensed something, and that's why I had to make you believe he was a fuck up artist."

Richie Rich was shocked to say the least as he looked over to Clyde and now remembered who he was, Chauncey's bum azz cousin, Kevin. Now he knew why he looked so familiar and why when he first seen him, Clyde said, "We finally meet again." Everything that was going on was so clear now, but Richie Rich hoped that his memory lapse didn't cause him, RJ, Jamillah, and their unborn child their lives.

"So, all this time, yo hoe azz was just waiting on yo chance to rob me, but for what? Three bricks?" Richie Rich frowned.

"It would've been just three slabs until you showed me what was behind that dummy wall, and that was too much merch for me not to make a play on, especially knowing how soft yo bitch azz is," Chauncey chuckled as Clyde came from the back of the house.

"Look what we got here," Clyde smiled as he placed both duffel bags on the living room floor and unzipped them to see the contents.

"We finna turn the fuck up," Gunna said while tugging on Jazzie's shoulder with excitement.

Looking around the room, depending on which side you were on, it was a sight to see. Richie Rich and RJ felt absolutely defeated while Chauncey and his people celebrated like they were having a jubilee.

Richie Rich looked over at his brother and sorrow immediately set in because he knew that if he had taken the time to really see what he was saying about not trusting Chauncey, then just maybe they wouldn't be staring death in the face. Richie then looked at Jamillah, and all he could do was close his eyes and feel remorseful for his childhood love as she sat vulnerable, molested, and disrespected. When Jamillah looked up and made eye contact with Richie, a slight chill shot through his body because they had beaten her until she was almost unrecognizable.

"What we gon' do about these muthafuckas?" Gunna asked.

"Shit, clean house and wipe they azzes down," Clyde replied while shrugging his shoulders.

Richie Rich knew the situation was about to get ugly, he just didn't know how ugly. He closed his eyes for a brief second to see if could utilize his ingenuity skills one last time to get him and his people out of this situation, then he heard a monstrous roar echo throughout the living room as if someone had just shot off a cannon twice. BOC! BOC!

Taken by surprise, Richie Rich opened his eyes and felt like his heart had just jumped out of his chest when he saw Clyde walk over and stand over RJ with his banger out.

RJ knew what was about to go down, but instead of tucking his tail, he had some shit to get off his chest.

"Fuck you faggot azz nigga, I'mma fuck all the bitches that died in yo family in they azz when I get ther..." RJ said but was cut off by Clyde raising his gun and firing three shots into RJ's chest. BOC! BOC! BOC!

"Noooooo!!" Richie Rich screamed as he watched the life leave out of his brother's body.

Richie Rich tried to get up, but his legs felt like noodles when he glanced over at Jamillah and realized that she had been shot, once in the head, and once in the chest as her body laid slumped sideways in the chair. All the feelings in his body left as rage set in, but for some reason he felt like he couldn't move. He tried to fight back his tears, but he couldn't contain them as they started falling rapidly. Richie Rich leaned back on the couch and realized his reality might be coming to an end. Gunna walked over shaking his head.

"Look at this nigga crying like a bitch."

"Fuck you pussy azz nigga, fuck all y'all," Richie Rich screamed as Chauncey walked over to him.

"I'll take that, but look at it like this, this is truly an I am my brother's keeper moment," Chauncey said while pointing his pistol in Richie Rich's face. "So I'mma ask you nigga ,am I my brother's keeper?" he added. Richie Rich didn't answer, he just stared at the floor in silence.

"Nuh uh, I'll meet y'all outside, I ain't staying in here for this," Jazzie stated.

"Me too," Bubbles agreed as she and Jazzie headed for the door while Chauncey continued to chastise Richie Rich.

"Now, where were we?" Chauncey said after the girls left. "I said am I my brother's keeper?" he continued in a loud aggressive tone, this time getting a reaction from Richie Rich.

"Hell naw!" Richie Rich screamed in anger. "You ain't never been shit but a lame azz bitch and that's all you'll ever be," he added.

"That's where you're wrong nigga, yes...I....am." BOC! He sent one .357 bullet ripping through Richie Rich's chest that sent him flying back into the couch before he slumped over and collapsed to the floor.

"Game over bitch nigga," Chauncey said, then turned toward Gunna, Schod, and Clyde. "Let's get the fuck outta here," he continued.

"Don't leave shit up in here," Clyde said while looking around making sure no evidence was left to link them to the bodies. After that, they left the house with the bags in their hands and made their way to Jazzie's house.

*****

The room was silent, death was apparent in the air as the sounds of an ambulance and police cars roared from a distance, cutting through a normally violent and drama filled night in the city of Milwaukee. Footsteps stampeded across the wooden floors as the police rushed into the house with their guns drew.

"They're in here!" the policeman yelled to the two paramedics after he and his partner made sure the rest of the house was secure. As the medics did their work, two homicide detectives entered the house. One went to peep the scene while the other approached one of the officers.

"What do we have here?" Detective Benson asked while looking around at the grewsome crime scene.

"Two D.O.A's and this fella here," the officer pointed to Richie Rich. "The medics say he has a severe gunshot wound to the chest. He lost a lot of blood, but they think he might make it," he added.

"Can he talk?" Benson asked the paramedics as they placed him on the gurney.

"I don't think so, we gotta get him outta here pronto if he's going to survive," the medic replied.

"Alright," Benson said as his partner walked up.

"I bet it was his own people that did this, they're always killing each oth..." he said but was cut off by the female medic turning to look at him before they wheeled Richie Rich off to the ambulance.

"This is a mess," Detective Benson said looking at Jamillah. "Make sure to take a photo of that bloody champagne bottle and send it to the lab for prints," he added.

"Will do, people are something else...geesh," his partner said.

"Don't start."

"Bet two boxes of donuts that I'm right."

Detective Benson disregarded his partner's irrational behavior, then he professionally responded, "I'll get the paperwork started," and walked off.

CHAPTER ELEVEN

"I told you that nigga was sweet, didn't I?" Chauncey said while getting out of the van.

"Sweet as bear meat." Gunna replied, grabbing one of the duffel bags while Clyde grabbed the other one before making their way to the house.

"Schod know what to do with the car right?" Chauncey asked. They had Schod go and dispose of Richie Rich's car.

"Yeah, fool gon' take the muthafucka on the South side and burn the bitch," Clyde said.

"Aight," Chauncey said content with his answer.

"Hold up, I know y'all ain't finna take that shit in my house," Jazzie said after getting out of her car.

"If you don't open this muthafucka up, we leavin' and we ain't comin' back. I don't know why you trippin', yo son ain't here...All that bogus azz shit you be doin' in that house," Clyde snapped.

"All we gon' do is count the money and split the shit up," Gunna chimed in.

"Why we can't do it somewhere else?"

"Aight fuck it, you must not want yo cut," Chauncey said, turning to leave as Gunna and Clyde did the same.

"Nigga don't play," she said putting her hand on her hip.

"Stop playin' then hoe and let us in before it rains," Bubbles said excitedly while wrapping her arms around Jazzie.

"Alright, but y'all ain't stayin' long," Jazzie stated while turning to walk up the porch.

"This hoe crazy," Clyde said shaking his head.

"Tell me about it," Gunna agreed as they walked up the steps.

Once they got in the house, they went into the living room and emptied the contents of both bags on the table. The scene was like a movie to them as they smiled gleefully.

"We finna eat my nigga," Chauncey said shaking up with Clyde as they stared at all the dope and money.

"On er'thang," Clyde replied as everybody else simultaneously reached for the money.

"Whoa whoa, y'all be easy," Chauncey said, stopping everybody from reaching. He knew he was in a room full of shiesty people and he couldn't allow nobody to be cuffin' shit on the low.

"If my math is right, we get about 75 thousand apiece," Jazzie said while picking up a pile of money to count.

"Put that shit down," Clyde said as he snatched the money from her hands and put it back on the table.

"Who gettin' 75 thousand apiece?" Chauncey asked with a bewildered look on his face. "You bitches ain't gettin' shit but 10 bands apiece, and the rest gettin' split up between us," he explained.

"You muthafuckas don' snapped, I took a risk just like y'all did. What if I would've gotten killed? Who was gon' take care of my son then?" Jazzie reasoned.

"I ain't tryna hear that shit, you knew what it was when you got involved. I'm the muthafucka that put the plan together and this part of the plan," Chauncey explained.

"Yeah, but I had to fuck his lil brother."

"Bitch beat it wit ya half slick azz, you was gon' fuck 'em anyway," Chauncey replied.

"Both you muthafuckas trippin', we still got all this dope to divide, so ain't no need for y'all to get out y'all bodies," Gunna stated.

"I don't sell no dope nigga! " Jazzie belted out. But when she saw Gunna shrug his shoulders as if he was saying, you'll just get the money then, she quickly spoke up. "But I will though."

Everybody smirked as Chauncey let out a light chuckle after hearing how fast Jazzie switched up what she was saying. Chauncey started pushing stacks of money in everyone's direction making sure they received their proper chop. He gave Bubbles and Jazzie 50 gees and a brick apiece and split the rest up three ways.

"I'm finna turn the TV on to see if they got anything on there about y'all boy," Clyde said while Chauncey kept dishing out the money...until BREAKING NEWS flashed across the screen which got everybody's attention as the news lady started talking.

"We're live on Milwaukee's north side where a heinous crime has just taken place. I'm told that there are deceased bodies inside, but it is unclear at this time how many victims are involved, the gender of those victims, or the motive, and there are no suspects in custody. Also, the chief of police will be holding a press conference first thing in the morning after he's briefed on this incident. As soon as more information is passed on to me, I will pass that on...Reporting live, this is Pamela Winfrey for Fox Milwaukee News."

Clyde turned the TV off and looked toward Chauncey.

"You a cold muthafucka," he said with a smile.

"I try to be, what can I say," Chauncey returned the smile. "Wit Richie Rich outta the way, we finna turn the fuck up in these streets and get this paper for real," he added.

"On er'thang," Clyde agreed.

"Now y'all get money by all means, but stay low. We don't need no heat after this one, that means you two go back to pussy poppin' or whatever y'all do at that club," Chauncey explained.

"Watch it nigga, don't be tryna get slick at the mouth because you got a few bands," Bubbles responded.

"Do what the fuck he said. You always runnin' yo slick azz mouth, but when you suckin' on this dick, you Ms. Can't Get Right," Gunna scolded her.

"You right, but how can I get right on some little shit like that?" Bubbles replied while pointing to his crotch area before turning to walk away. "Come on girl, let's go," she continued.

"I'm not leaving these crazy azz niggas in my house," Jazzie said.

"We finna get up outta here anyway, there's a new king bout to be crowned in Milwaukee," Chauncey stated smiling.

"I'm finna hit it back to the East and see if I can get some of this work off," Gunna said.

"Y'all just remember to stay low," Chauncey insisted, looking around at everybody making sure they got his drift.

"Let's just take two bricks apiece then, ain't no need to be driving across town with all that bullshit," Clyde said logically.

"Shid, I'm takin' all mine wit me. That's not what I meant when I said stay low key. I got traps that's gon' pump this shit right out," Chauncey said, knowing he wouldn't look too suspicious because Richie Rich was his right-hand man and niggas already thought he was having money. Besides, he wasn't thrilled about leaving his work at Jazzie's house because he knew money was the root of all evil and she was liable to get ghost with his shit.

"Well I can't take all mine right now?" Gunna said.

"Y'all ain't finna keep that shit here," Jazzie stated.

"How about we give you two gees to leave it here until tomorrow," Gunna said.

"Apiece," she bargained with her hand out.

"You something else." Clyde shook his head as he and Gunna gave her two thousand dollars apiece.

"So, we good now?" Gunna asked.

"We excellent," she said cuffing the money.

"I'mma get up wit y'all later," Chauncey said after zipping up the bag with his money and dope before throwing it over his shoulder. "Now don't do no stupid shit that's gon' cause any attention, y'all be easy," he added before leaving out the door after giving everybody a fist pound.

Jazzie went to stash her money and all the dope. When she returned, Gunna and Clyde were already gone, so she held the door open for Bubbles, then followed her to the car where they hopped in, and pulled off.

CHAPTER TWELVE

(Two months later)

"Noooo!" BOC! BOC! BOC! Richie Rich tossed and turned. He had awoken to a flashback of the worst night of his life. As his adrenaline pumped, his heart rate accelerated which caused the respirator to start going crazy.

"Jamillah," he whispered under his breath. "RJ, nawww man naw," he added as tears started running down his face."Noooo!" he continued yelling as a nurse entered the room and woke him up.

"Sir! Sir!" she yelled trying to get him to snap out of it. Richie Rich opened his eyes and looked around the unfamiliar room until he locked eyes with the nurse.

"Where am I?" he asked as he tried to sit up, but quickly laid back down when the sharp pains pierced across his chest."Ahhh!" he moaned out in obvious pain as the nurse put a straw in the cup and let him drink some water as a second nurse entered the room.

"I see your back with us," she smiled. "Do you know who you are?" she added.

"How long have I been here?" he inquired.

"Sixty-two days."

"What?"

"Yep, you were in a coma, so I need to know do you know who you are?" she asked, following her routine line of questions while pulling out a small flashlight and checking both of his eyes.

"Yeah."

"Who?" she asked, wanting conformation that he was conscious and aware.

"Richard... Richard Williams."

*****

(Five days later)

Richie Rich parked his tinted up Chevy Trailblazer, pulled his Milwaukee Bucks fitted cap low on his head, and peeped the scenery before he exited the truck and walked through the gang way.

About 20 minutes after he came out of the coma, two homicide detectives entered his hospital room asking him numerous questions about the night his brother, girlfriend, and their unborn child lost their lives. So, Richie Rich acted as if this was something random and faked ignorance to the situation. The detectives knew he was lying, but they couldn't do anything about it, so Richie Rich knew he had to be extra careful and calculate his steps well, because he didn't know if they were following him or not.

Richie Rich used his key and entered the house through the back door. He slowly walked to the room that he used to share with Jamillah and looked around shaking his head knowing his carelessness ultimately cost him her life as well as RJ's. Richie Rich flipped the picture frame on the wall back and entered the code to the small wall safe. Inside was 20 thousand dollars cash, his "Garfield" chain, two glock 9mm's, a couple Rolex's, and Jamillah's jewelry.

He grabbed the cash and both guns before locking the safe and flipping the picture back. When he made it to the living room, he saw yellow police tape and outlines of where Jamillah and RJ died. The thick plush carpeting was stained in blood and Richie Rich started to get emotional as tears fell from his eyes

His heart rate quickened causing his chest to hurt. Digging in his pocket, he grabbed the pill bottle and put two OxyContin's in his mouth and swallowed them dry before dropping to his knees.

"Why!!" he screamed before he looked down. He had allowed not only the streets, but his best friend to prey on him. They stripped him of not only his woman and brother, but of fatherhood as well. He reminisced over all the times in his life when people treated him, took his shit, and he didn't do anything about it. Thinking of all of that, something in him snapped. He was no longer going to be the prey he was going to be the hunter, he was sick of crying and everybody that was responsible for his sorrow and pain would pay with their lives. Richie Rich looked up with a devilish grin on his face ready to do what had to be done and reclaim what was his by any means necessary.

*****

(Two days later)

"Peaches bring yo big booty azz over here."

"What nigga?" she walked up and leaned over the table, just inches from his face.

"Let me get a dance" he said, but when he seen her face, he knew it was a no go since he stuck his finger in her ass the last time. So, before she could turn him down, he switched it up. "Tell 'ol girl to come holla at me!" he pointed. Peaches turned to see who he was talking about. "What's her name again?" he added.

"Stop playin' dumb, you know her name, all y'all black azz niggas know," Peaches said, hatin' like a muthafucka.

"Well tell her that Chauncey requests her presence," he said then made a gesture with his hand as if he was shooing her, but she caught him when she turned her head back around.

"Nuh uh, don't be tryna shoo me because you got a lil money now. I don't know who you used to fuckin' wit but I ain't that bitch," she stated in a sassy tone.

"I'm what's hat-nen around these ways baby girl, I know you can see that," he said, looking himself up and down. "Now get over there and tell 'ol girl to come holla at me and maybe later on I'll throw you a band or two to bounce that big ass on this dick," he added confidently

"Really! Who said I want that dick inside me?" she asked.

"Jackson's, Grant's, and Franklin's," he said while digging in his pocket.

"Who?"

"Twenty's, Fifty's, Hundreds," he said passing her a knot then smacking her on the ass.

"You a mess," she smiled, accepting the money before turning to leave. She pranced over to Val as Chauncey sat back and watched her whisper in her ear.

Val smiled with a giggle making Chauncey curious to know what she was saying about him. When Val cut her eyes in his direction, he flared his chest out and looked off to the side as if he wasn't paying her any attention.

Peaches then walked toward the back as Val made her way over to Chauncey. He relaxed and tried to have some extra drip to his sauce when he noticed her coming in his direction. Val's body was a piece of art and she had one of the baddest walks he'd ever seen, the way her hips swayed, her thick thighs contracted with every step, and her D- cup breasts that would bounce. The bald head hairstyle only complimented the features in her face and made her light blue eyes stick out.

"What can I do for you?" she asked while placing her hands on her hips, sticking her ass out, and standing as if she was pigeon toed.

"I'm tryna get a few lap dances from the best in this place."

"I'm sorry boo boo, I was just about to leave, I got other plans tonight," she said, noticing the lustful look in his eyes. From the way he looked at her, she knew that if she wanted him, he'd be just another sucka in her stable.

"I know you ain't finna turn all this money down," he said pulling out a large wad of rubber banded money. She could see that he had his bands up, but she was not thirsty so she knew better than to go on the first try. She was all about playing her cards right.

"Listen, if your money's not in my pocket, someone else's will be as long as I can do this," she said, turning around and making each ass cheek jump individually. "I'll produce money whenever I want to, but don't trip, I'll catch up with you later," she added while rubbing his bald head before turning to leave.

She knew Chauncey was hooked and couldn't keep his eyes off of her, so she emphasized her strut while gliding across the room. She quickly turned her head and caught him damn near hypnotized. She winked at him then whispered "Got 'em" to herself. Knowing it was only a matter of time before she had her hands permanently in his pockets.

"Damn," Chauncey said under his breath while imagining his dick in between her big white butt cheeks. He knew that his imagination would soon turn into a reality, so he wasn't trippin' as he downed the rest of his drink, threw a twenty on the table, and left outta P.T.'s to go meet up with one of his boys who was trying to cop a half brick.

*****

"Hello," Clyde said answering his ringing cellphone.

"What up boy?"

"Shit, what's good my dude?"

"Meet me at Jazzie crib in 30 minutes, I'm finna catch this quick action and then I'm on my way," Gunna said.

"Fo sho, I'm on the same shit so 30 minutes is perfect," Clyde laughed.

"I'mma holla then, luv."

"Luv."

Gunna hung up his cellphone and turned into the parking lot to the food place on 27th and Fond du Lac. He checked the clock on his phone, and it was a little after 9:30pm. He wondered where the nigga was that he was supposed to be meeting, but no longer than he thought it, a black Grand Prix pulled up next to him with two dudes inside. Gunna pulled his .40 Baretta out and sat it on his lap.

The passenger got out and walked around their car as Gunna lowered his window.

"What's up fam?" Big Mike said.

"What's good Big Mike, get in," Gunna said before he covered the gun with his shirt for precautionary reasons. He was on a main street that was well lit, so he figured he should be good. "You got that cash fam?" he added, getting straight down to business while paying close attention to Big Mike's every movement because he knew how the game was played in certain situations like this, so he thought.

"I got 26 bands right here" Big Mike said holding up a brown paper bag. "They still 13 apiece right?" he added.

"Yeah, I'm just tryna dump this shit off."

"Aight, where it at?" Big Mike asked ready to get up outta there knowing the police could pull up any minute on that hot azz strip.

"I got you right here." Gunna reached under his seat and pulled out two heavily duct taped kilos while trying his best to conceal the pistol. He sat the brick on his lap, but kept one hand under his shirt. Needless to say, he was completely out of his element or he would've known not to be selling that much weight that late at night.

"Looks good to me," Big Mike said, opening the bag, reaching in, and pulling out some of the money to start counting. He kept watching Gunna out of his peripheral vision while he shuffled through the bills to see if he noticed the swift movement that just occurred.

"No need for that fam, you good," Gunna said, feeling uneasy and eager to get on his way before the police rolled up because they looked suspicious.

As Big Mike handed the bag to Gunna, he started asking him irrelevant questions as a distraction. Gunna never seen the driver of the Grand Prix get out and sneak up on his driver's side window. Unaware of his demise, Gunna grabbed the money and started to hand over the bricks when he heard.

"Say partna!"

Caught by surprise, Gunna looked up startled. He knew he was in a no win situation, but he refused to go out like that. As he reached for his heat, the Grand Prix driver filled him with four slugs. BOC! BOC! BOC! BOC!

*****

Clyde pulled up in front of Jazzie's house and realized Gunna hadn't made it there yet, so he parked and called his phone several times resulting in the voicemail every time.

Clyde got outta the car and went to retrieve the spare key that Jazzie had secretly placed above the light on her porch. She didn't know he knew about it, but he'd seen Gunna do this numerous times when Jazzie wasn't home.

Clyde put the key back, but left the door unlocked thinking that he'd just come in, wait on Gunna, they'd grab the work, and be up outta there before Jazzie ever knew they were there. He turned on the living room light, sat on the couch, grabbed the remote control to the stereo, and turned on "What if" by Kevin Gates. He started rolling up some kush to relax until his boy showed up. About five minutes into his session, his phone rung.

"Hello," he leaned back on the couch pulling hard on the blunt.

"Where you at? I got this dude tryna get right," Jazzie said, letting Clyde know she knew somebody who was tryna cop some work.

"Don't worry bout my whereabouts, money all I care about," he laughed.

"Whateva nigga, where you at though?" she asked.

"At yo crib."

"How the fuck you get in my shit?"

"I'm waiting on Gunna so we can get the rest of that shit out yo house, so whoever dude is, tell 'em it's gon' be about an hour."

"That's cool, y'all hurry up and get the fuck out my house too, and don't be in there smellin' a bitch panties neither," she laughed before Clyde cut her off.

"Whatever bitch," Clyde said and hung the phone up. He took a few more totes on the blunt before he changed the music to this mixed tape called "I Love Haters" by this up and coming rapper outta Milwaukee by the name of Party Boi. Turning up the song titled "I fuck wit em" featuring Amazing, he rapped along with the chorus..

"Bad bitches I fuck wit em/ Real niggas I fuck wit em/ No fuck niggas no fuck bitches/can't keep it 100 I can't fuck wit em..."

Clyde was one, getting lost in the moment. He closed his eyes while rapping word for word with the song, when all of a sudden, he felt a piece of steel pressed against his forehead. He opened his eyes and it was on like he seen a ghost. His jaw dropped and with a dumb azz look on his face. He said, "I got yo shit right here man," in a pleading tone. Karma was an ugly bitch and Clyde knew he was about to marry her. "It's all here I promise," he continued while looking into Richie Rich's eyes. Clyde realized by the look in Richie Rich's eyes, that all the pleading he was doing fell upon deaf ears. Clyde kept his hands up high while he proceeded to try and convince Richie Rich that it wasn't his idea and that he would make sure he got all of his merch back. Richie Rich stared at him with no emotions and asked him in a calm tone.

"So, you gon' give me everything, back right?"

"Yeah man everything, I got you," he responded sorrowfully.

"What about my lady, my baby, and my brother?" Richie asked coyly. Clyde had no answer for that question, so Richie Rich slapped him across the face with his pistol. SMACK! "I can't hear you muthafucka," he added.

"Man, I swear on my mama I..." he started to say before Richie Rich cut him off.

"Open yo muthafuckin' mouth."

"I'm sorry man, I swear I didn't..." he tried to speak.

"I said open yo muthafuckin' mouth and I ain't gon' say it again," Richie Rich said in a low growl. Clyde tried to act tough, but his emotions got the best of him and he started to cry because he knew the reaper was close and he was there to take his soul. He attempted to speak again, and Richie popped him. BOC!

"Arrghh, fuck!" Clyde yelled after getting shot in the knee. When he opened his mouth, Richie Rich pushed the hot pistol in on an upward angle so that it was pressing against the roof of his mouth. Then he leaned over him, grabbed the back of his head, pulled it forward, and with pure malice, he told him, "Life is like an echo. Sometimes what you send out comes back." Then, he pulled the trigger. BOC! The large caliber bullet knocked a hole in the top of his head the size of a cantaloupe as he fell back on the couch with his eyes open.

*****

"Hello"

"Schod where the fuck yo big head Shawty lo lookin' azz at,me and Tez waiting on yo slow azz!" Shay yelled into the phone.

"I just came from gettin' my car washed, I'm finna pull up to the crib and get dressed and I'll be there in less than a half hour," Schod said.

"Man hurry up, and don't come over here wit them same azz Robin's you had on the last two times we went out either," Shay laughed.

"You a muthafuckin' lie, you just pick that afro on that one side that's always on flat," Schod said as they laughed.

"Fuck you, and hurry yo azz up," Shay responded before ending the call. Schod had been doing good in the streets since Chauncey gave him a brick and 30 gees for coming through for him the night of the robbery. He copped a new Infiniti on chrome '24 Rucci rims, and had been checkin' a heavy bag in. Schod rapped along with Milwaukee's own Larry Byrds as he turned into the alley of his safe house on 19th and Hampton and parked on the slab in the back of his house. Getting out of the car, he hit the alarm, and walked to his backdoor. As soon as he put his key in the door, he heard something coming from the bushes that didn't seem normal and his survival intuition told him that somebody was over there. He needed to get his strap, but as soon as he reached for it, it was too late, as a barrage of bullets flew in his direction BOC! BOC! BOC! BOC! BOC! BOC! BOC! BOC! BOC! BOC! BOC! BOC! BOC! BOC!

"Don't worry about who the fuck I am," Richie Rich said while stepping out of the bushes, tucking his pistol, and then he took off running. He stated that to a dead Schod because that's what he told him the night they tried to kill him.

*****

"Damn girl, where you been the last couple of months? P.T. been asking about you and Jazzie," Peaches said in a curious tone whole looking in her eyes tryna get a read on her. "Matter of fact, where is that hoe Jazzie?" she added.

"I don't know. She was supposed to meet me here, but she claim she got some business to take care of first with some dude, and then she'll be on her way," Bubbles stated.

"What! She hoein' now?"

"Hell naw bitch, you trippin' now. She just got business to attend to, but I see you still nosey as hell," Bubbles said in a sassy tone.

"Somethings never change," Peaches laughed.

"Is Val still working here, I haven't seen her in a while, ever since..." Bubbles paused as she flashed back to the night they were at Richie Rich's house before she caught herself. "Nevermind, but is she here though?" she continued.

"Yeah girl she still work here, that hoe on her paper too. You know how these niggas get when they see a white bitch with a big booty and got a little game about herself, these niggas be goin' nuts and forget about where they came from," she said with envy dripping from her tone.

Just to humor herself, Bubbles asked, "Where they come from girl?"

"The motherland!" she replied as Bubbles busted into laughter.

"Girl please, where she at?"

"She ain't here right now, she said she had something to do," Peaches said. "Oh yeah, guess who was in here sweatin' the shit out that bitch earlier?" she added.

"Who?"

"Shitty finger azz Chauncey," Peaches stated.

"For real" Bubbles replied as if she hadn't seen him in a while.

"That's a weird azz nigga if I ever seen one. What normal muthafucka you know stick they finger in a bitch ass that they don't even know like that? Most niggas try to slide in the pussy, but the ass? Girl he got tendency's I'm tellin' you," Peaches said as they both started laughing hysterically, then Bubbles cellphone rang.

"Where you at?" she answered in a high pitch tone. Then, she rolled her eyes and turned her back when she noticed Peaches all in her mouth.

"I gotta run to my house real quick to grab something, so I'll be there in twenty minutes tops," Jazzie explained.

"I'm not about to be waiting here all day."

"You act like you got something better to do, just pop that musty azz pussy of yours until I get there. You know how to make money," Jazzie giggled with a smile plastered on her face.

"No, you didn't. Suck a dick bitch," she shot back playfully laughing as well.

"Maybe tonight, but I love you too." Then, she hung up.

"Who was that?" Peaches said when Bubbles turned back around with her face scrunched up. She retracted her question. "Never mind," she added.

"You finally catching on."

CHAPTER THIRTEEN

"What the fuck is this nigga still doin' at my house?" Jazzie questioned to herself when she turned the corner and saw Clyde's van still parked out front. When she pulled up and looked toward her house, she noticed her living room curtains were slightly open and stained with something red.

"Oh hell naw, I just bought them cream curtains and this fool spilled something on 'em, he finna gimme my five-hundred dollars back," she added as she got out of the car and walked toward the porch. When she got closer, she seen what looked like hamburger meat splashed against the window which pissed her off even more as she opened the door and yelled.

"Clyde, you finna pay me for my curtains, you..." she said walking into the living room to something she had only seen in movies."AAaahhhh!" she screamed as her purse and keys fell to the floor then she covered her mouth. "What the fuck!" she continued as she walked toward him calling his name in a low whisper hoping that he was still alive. But once she was close enough to see the top part of his head was gone, she started having convulsions, then she panicked, and quickly dialed 9-1-1.

After reporting Clyde's death, she hung up, and quickly called Gunna, but his phone kept sending her to voicemail, so she left him a text saying, "Clyde's dead at my house." Then, she walked to the front door and put her back against the wall. She couldn't stand being in the same room while someone she considered family laid in a pool of blood with his head opened. She attempted to call Chauncey four times, and he finally answered on the fifth.

"What up girl?" he asked.

"He dead, Chauncey. Somebody killed Clyde!" she cried out in a shivering voice and wouldn't stop babbling on until he spoke up.

"Who killed cuz?"

"I don't know. I came home and he was on my couch dead. I need you to come over here now," she explained.

"Aight, I'm just gettin' off the interstate comin' from the Chi as we speak, I'm on my way so just be patient and don't do nothing until I get there."

Still crying and sobbing, she said, "I called 9-1-1 already and they should be here in a minute," while looking out the window in both directions to see if the police or ambulance had arrived.

"Awww fuck,a in't that shit still in the house?"

"He told me y'all was coming to get it out."

"Who told you that?"

"Clyde nigga, who else?" she yelled through the phone.

"Well obviously he ain't make it out, so you betta check before them people get there," he said in a concerned tone. "Hit me back and let me know what up," he added.

"Okay," she said hanging up. She walked back into the living room and looked at Clyde. The way his body was slumped over. She noticed the bulge in his side, so she lifted his shirt and grabbed the glock 20 that was in his waistband with the intention of stashing it before the cops came. She frantically dashed into her son's room and grabbed the four bricks that was hidden in his toy box. Then, she ran from room to room to see if Gunna had stashed anything in a place she didn't know about. Seeing nothing, she ran back toward the living room wiping tears away with the back of her hand. She held the pistol in one hand and had the bricks cradled in her other hand, she was caught off guard by a commanding voice that scared her.

"Freeze, Police, don't move!" Still in a state of shock, she dropped the dope, and lifted the gun swinging it around toward the screaming voice. "Gun, gun, drop the gun!" BOC! BOC!

She hit the floor with a thump as one of the police officers ran over and kicked the gun away. The officer kneeled down and lifted her head to stop her from choking on her own blood. She coughed then whispered.

"My...my....tell him...tell him....I....I....I love.... Tell my son...ple.." then she gasped for one last breath.

The officer checked her pulse, looked up toward his partner, and shook his head.

"She gone!"

*****

"Damn, where this bitch at, talkin' bout she gon' be here in twenty minutes," Bubbles said to herself while walking out to the main floor. It was packed wall to wall tonight. She thought about working, but decided against it. She couldn't even make it past the first table before Peaches spotted her and walked over.

"She still ain't here yet? That bitch must be hoein' because she always wanna shake her ass."

"You always got some slick shit to say. Everybody don't feel like havin' all them niggas hands on their body everyday coppin' free feels tryna stick their fingers in yo pussy on the sneak tip as they cram $10 dollars down yo thong, but you on the other hand, hmm..." Bubbles rolled her eyes.

"What that supposed to mean?"

"Hoe you know, wit yo flat backin' azz."

"Well I'm not gon' have all this foreva," she said running her hands up and down her body. "So you can hate all you want, but I gotta have mine," she added. Peaches' voice became distant to Bubbles as she zoned out and stopped paying her antics any attention as she pulled out her cellphone and called Jazzie. *Got me waitin', listening to this stupid azz bitch, where the hell you at?* she thought to herself while the phone was ringing. Getting no answer, she decided to leave.

As she was making her way to the exit, Peaches called her name, but she ignored her and kept walking toward the door. Looking outside, she saw that it was raining cats and dogs and all she had on was a wife beater with no bra, a pair of booty shorts that had the bottom of her cheeks hanging out in the back, and a pair of open toe Fendi sandals.

"I know you ain't finna drive in that," Peaches said, walking up behind her noticing that the rain was coming down.

"Damn bitch, I thought I left yo azz ova there," she stated when she saw Peaches looking over her shoulder.

"I'm just saying girl, it's raining like a muthafucka out there. You might as well stay and get this money." Peaches said

"You see this bitch, I got it," she said, opening her purse and pulling out five gees just to shut Peaches up.

"What's that?"

"Money hoe, something you ain't got a lot of."

"Bitch that ain't no money."

"That's funny bitch wit yo broke azz. You in this muthafucka all day every day and you ain't even copped a decent whip. You losin' and on that note, I'm outta here," she turned with her purse held over her head and ran to her car. She fumbled with the keys before she finally got the door opened and slid in. She turned to put her purse down on the passenger seat when she saw what seemed to be a shadow out of her peripheral vision, when all of a sudden an arm wrapped around her neck and squeezed. As she was getting choked and gasping for air, she managed to look in her rearview mirror, and into the eyes of Richie Rich.

"You thought I was dead didn't you bitch," he said in a low raspy voice as he tightened his grip around her neck. She gagged and fought for her life while she kept hitting his arm with one hand and pushing the horn with the other one trying to get someone's attention. She kicked and jerked her body, but it was all for nothing because his grip was too tight. "You ain't gon' ever get a chance to fuck nobody else ova," he said leaning back and tightening up his grip until he felt the air leave her body. When she went limp, he reached in her purse, grabbed the five bands, got out of the car, and disappeared into the night.

*****

When Jazzie didn't call him back, his mind started racing, so he decided to play it from a distance when he got to her house to check the scene out. He tried calling Bubbles on his way over there, but there was no answer.

"Where the fuck everybody at?" he said to himself worriedly. He tried calling Gunna but didn't get an answer, then he called Jazzie and still no answer. "This shit crazy," he added.

His heart started racing when he turned the corner to Jazzie's block and quickly pulled over by the corner in his tinted up minivan after he seen an ambulance, three squad cars, and two detective cars parked outside her house with crime scene tape wrapped around her shit like a Christmas present. He leaned back and put his hands on the top of his head and said.

"This can't be happening."

He contemplated on leaving, but decided to wait and see what developed, so he leaned back and waited. Ten minutes later the coroner's van pulled up and went inside. Chauncey sat up to see what transpired next. He already knew Clyde was dead because Jazzie told him, but he didn't know what happened to Jazzie. He didn't see anyone in the back of the squad cars, so he assumed she left with the dope and money. A few minutes later, the two coroners came out carrying a body bag.

"Damn, that must be Clyde," he told himself while watching them put the body bag in the back of the coroner's van and then they returned into the house. Chauncey shook his head because his Auntie was going to be heart broken by his cousin's death. He was just about to pull off when he seen the coroner's come out carrying another body bag. He exhaled then closed his eyes and whispered to himself.

"Who the fuck is that?"

After sitting there confused, he finally came to his senses, backed up to the next block, took one last look, and smashed off.

*****

"Hello," she said answering her ringing cellphone.

"What's been going on wit you?"

"Shit, just doin' me as always, why what up?"

"Tryna get myself back in the game, that's all," he said smoothly.

"I was wondering where you disappeared to."

"You don't even know who you talkin' too, do you?" he said sternly.

"The hell if I don't, that aggressive attitude and voice get me hot and bothered every time I hear it," she said as they laughed. "For a minute I thought you forgot about me," she added.

"Not at all, you remember when I told you I was gon' need you to do something for me down the line?"

"Yeah," she said with excitement.

"I'mma need to cash in on that, aight."

"Can I at least get a sample of that thang you toting around before we do business?"

He paused for a minute then said, "Here's the address, call me when you get out front, come by yourself, and don't tell nobody where you goin', Aight." he said then hung up.

After hearing the click in her ear, she looked at her cellphone with the expression on her face like "No he didn't just hang up on me," but she was secretly head over heels about his sauce, he had it drippin',so she jumped in the shower, threw on her freak 'em dress, jumped in her car, and said to herself, "I gotta have me some of this man," as she started the car and sped off.

CHAPTER FOURTEEN

"Who is it?" Richie Rich said through the phone trying to disguise his voice.

"Val."

"Aight, I'm on my way down," he said while getting up, sliding on his shirt, and tucking his pistol in his waistband. Making his way down the hallway to the front of his apartment complex, he saw Val standing outside the door strapped to death, he shook his head because he knew where this was going to lead no matter what he thought as he opened the door.

"I see you finally made it, what took you so long?" he cut into her.

"Damn! Well hello to you too. I just don't go anywhere lookin' like anything, I had to get myself together before I came to see you," she stated. "Now can I come in or are you gonna leave all this standing out here," she added, looking herself up and down.

Richie Rich couldn't do anything but smile at her sassiness as he stepped to the side and let her pass. She smelled of the new Chanel No.5 perfume which made him smile, then he peeked out into the night to make sure she was alone and not followed.

After he shut the door, he turned around to see her adjusting her all black form fitting thigh high dress with the short laced sleeves and matching 3inch Christian Louboutin platform pumps.

"You got a staring problem," she smiled, knowing she was turning him on. Richie Rich didn't reply, he just directed her toward his apartment. Val put an extra umph in her step making her ass swing because she knew he was watching and all Richie Rich could think about was that Ty Dolla $ign and Meek Mill song "Watching" as Val snapped him outta his trance. "You like what you see back there?" she asked while looking over her shoulder.

Richie Rich paused for a second then replied, "You straight, it's that last apartment on the right." He didn't want his compliments to go to her head, so he kept them to a minimum even though she was bad.

"When he opened the door, the only things that occupied the apartment was a let out couch, a 20" flat screen TV, and a DVD player that sat on a table with a CD player next to it.

"Damn, I see you brought me to a spot," Val stated.

"It ain't even like that, this one of my duck off spots," he assured her. "Plus we here to discuss business, so you good," he added as he made his way over to turn down "Light Work"by up and coming Milwaukee artist, Rob Dolla. "You want somethin' to sip or smoke on?" he continued, heading to the kitchen.

"Suck on," she said low enough that he didn't hear her. Richie Rich came back with a fifth of Remy Rosé, an ounce of moon rock, and sat 'em both on the table. Val picked the bottle up, read the label, looked at him, and said, "Brown make me wanna get down."

"Oh yeah," he laughed and handed her a box of Dutch blunts. "Roll this up," he added.

"It's finna be a party up in this bitch and I'm glad we're the only two attending."

"It's gon' stay like that. I'm cuttin' muthafuckas off and tightening my circle up," he expressed.

"Yeah, I heard about you," she said setting flame to the blunt.

"What you hear?" he asked curious to know what the streets had been talking about while he was outta commission, then he took a large gulp of the liquor.

"That somebody killed you, but I felt that wasn't true because we still haven't gotten properly acquainted with each other, so I'm glad to see that wasn't true, " she paused. "Let me get some of that," she reached out to grab the bottle from him. She took two long puffs from the blunt, passed it to him, then she grabbed the neck of the bottle and swallowed a large portion of the bottle and handed it back to him.

"Damn!" he said looking at the bottle sideways because he had never seen a chick get down on a bottle like that, then he looked at her as she wiped her mouth.

"What can I say, a bitch got a deep throat," she smiled while running her index finger around her lips before she sucked on it while staring in his eyes letting him know that she wanted to suck on something else. Changing the subject, Richie Rich tried to run his objective by her.

"Check it out, I'mma need you to fuck this nigga mind up so that I can get close to him. He got a thang for strippers and you one of the best in the game right now, so I know you can pull it off," he said, knowing it wasn't too many white girls built like her that niggas wouldn't be sweating.

"It's a lot I can pull off," she said, trying to entice him to come off some of his meat.

"I'm sure it is," he agreed looking at her sexy azz as the liquor took its effect.

"I'mma do what you asked me to do, so feel special because I never do that for anybody." She scooted over closer to him. "Now can I get what I been waiting for?" she added.

"If you insist," he replied.

Val stood from the couch, reached around, unzipped her dress, and let it fall to the floor. Richie Rich stood up, pulled out the bed, and sat on it while watching her standing there completely naked. Val made one ass cheek jump, then the other one before making them jump at the same time as she looked over her shoulder at Richie Rich's lustful gaze while he enjoyed the show.

Val turned around displaying perfectly shaped double D-cup breasts with hard pink pierced nipples that looked like bullets, a flat stomach, and a cleanly shaven pussy.

Richie Rich leaned back and glided his hand over his crotch trying to keep it cool, but he knew he was about to beat that pussy into a coma as she slowly crawled on the bed like a cat, flipped on her back with her legs spread, and showed off the fattest pussy lips that he had ever seen.

"Damn," he tried to whisper, but she heard him. She smiled as she used her index and middle finger to part her juicy lower lips showing its pink filling.

Richie Rich couldn't take it no more. He jumped up, pulled his shirt off, then his pants and boxers.

"Ummm, that's what I'm talkin' about," she said after seeing his 9" inches dangling from in between his legs. He grabbed a Magnum from his pants pocket and slid it down as far as it would go. Getting in the bed, he positioned his body over hers, and put one of her legs around his arm, then Val released herself to him when she said, "It's all yours daddy."

Richie Rich fingered her until she was nice and wet, then slowly pushed the head in, and watched her pussy lips hug his dick like a glove as she let out a passionate moan.

"Oohhh, push it all the way in daddy, beat this pussy up," she purred out.

In one powerful thrust he drove in balls deep inside, stretching her pussy to capacity as her juices rolled down his pipe with every stroke. Val had her eyes closed in a sexual trance as she moaned while clawing at his back.

Richie Rich had to admit that she had a good shot, but he didn't say a word, he just put his dick game down the best way he knew how. About 15 minutes into their session, Val was sucking on her tittie and fidgeting at her clitoris as she came for the first time.

"Ohh my gawd...I'm...cummin'," she moaned. Richie Rich felt like he was on the verge of cummin' himself, but he wanted to see how the pussy was from the back, so he pulled out, slung her leg over to the side, and smacked her hard on the ass. Val already knew what time it was as she flipped over, got face down ass up, and reached around spreading her cheeks wide open.

"Any hole you want baby," she whispered.

Richie Rich mounted her from the back, slid back into the pussy, and stroked her four times before he pulled out and used his dick to moisten her ass hole with her pussy juices. Then he slid into her winking ass hole slowly. Val grabbed the pillow and bit down into it as she accepted all that he had to give. He would come out far enough so only the head was in before he'd go all the way in making his balls slap against her pussy.

"Ohh yesss....oh ummm...give me that big black dick!" she yelled.

Watching her ass jump and bounce around with every thrust, Richie Rich couldn't take it anymore and with one last thrust, he shot his load, and immediately was spent as he stood up.

"That's one thing about you black muthafuckas, y'all sholl know how to fuck," she said.

"And white bitches know how to suck the dicks," he retorted.

"You ain't neva lied," she said crawling to the edge of the bed, grabbing his dick with her hands, and then pulled the rubber off, wrapped her lips around it, and swallowed it to the base. Richie Rich grabbed the back of her head and said, "Damn girl," while he enjoyed her excellent fellatio skills. She licked up the underside of his shaft and put his balls in her mouth before putting his member back in her mouth while slurping and sucking aggressively.

Feeling his second nut nearing, Richie Rich snatched his dick outta her mouth and jagged it off as Val held her tongue out waiting on his baby making batch. When he exploded, it splashed all over her face and chest, then he put it back in her mouth to let her suck the rest out. As Val sucked, something happened to abruptly cause her to stop.

"Ohh you got it in my nose and in my eye and it's burnin'," she said getting out of the bed. "I'll be right back," she added before running to the bathroom.

Richie Rich chuckled as he watched the thick tanned white chick trot across the room with ass and titties bouncing everywhere. Grabbing a towel to wipe the sweat from his body.

Richie Rich would be lying if he said he wasn't exhausted, he thought about calling it a night and having Val spend the night so he could beat that up until the sun woke up, but he knew he had a bigger task at hand and that task was revenge, so he got dressed, grabbed the blunt, and fired it up.

As he smoked, Val came from the bathroom with a towel wrapped around her, he could tell that she had just got out of the shower. Walking seductively toward the bed, she reached down to grab her dress with her ass facing him so he could get one last glimpse of her sweet, sweet pussy from the back.

"Now that we got that outta the way, we can handle this other business."

"I hope we can do it again some time, but tell me what you had in mind again," she said, letting out a school girl giggle. The dick had her feeling good.

"It's simple, I want you to seduce this dude, bring him back here, do the same thing to him that you just did to me, and I'll handle the rest," he explained.

"You want me to fuck him, so I'm yo hoe now?" she asked in disbelief.

"Believe me when I say it won't even get that far," he assured her while he sat on the let out bed, slid his feet into his retro '96 Nike Air Griffey Max, and tied them up.

"Whatever you say, but don't think just because you dicked me down that you got me in yo front pocket," she said. But deep down inside, she knew that was exactly how it was as she grabbed his arm, sat down next to him, and put her head on his shoulder.

"I don't know what type of niggas you used to fuckin' wit, but I can assure you that I ain't one of 'em. After we handle this business and I pay you, you can get the fuck on, that's yo choice," he said, putting everything on the wood.

"You right, so who is this dude you want me to get for you?" she asked, unfazed by his boldness.

"Chauncey."

"Hold up, ain't that the dude you used to hang with?" she asked curiously.

"Naw, I don't fuck wit 'em and when you wit him don't mention my name," he paused. Val knew for a fact that he used to hang with Chauncey. They dropped her off at the strip club the night her and Bubbles did the private party for them. She wondered why he would lie about that, and she also wondered did he have something to do with Richie getting shot. She didn't speak on it, but it was all on her mind. "And since you know who he is, you shouldn't have a problem seducing that clown, right?" he added.

"He be in the club sweating the shit outta me, so it definitely won't be a problem. He might be at the club right now," Val retorted, getting Richie Rich's full attention.

"You think so?"

"Yeah, he always there and if he is, I got 'em," she stated.

"Go check it out and I'mma be here, but if he is still there call me when you're on your way. If not, just hit me tomorrow and let me know what up, aight."

"I got you," she said grabbing her purse and making her way to the door before turning around. "If he don't show, I'mma still hit you up tonight. I got a few more rounds in me," she added smiling.

"Fo sho," he said returning the smile while walking her out to the main door.

CHAPTER FIFTEEN

*P*ulling up to the club, Val sat for a minute going over the steps of what she needed to do. She really hoped he didn't show so she could go back and get her back blown out, but if he did show, she'd have everything under control. She exited the car and walked toward the club where she was met by a frantic Peaches.

"Girl where the fuck you been? All type of shit been going on," Peaches exclaimed.

"Why, what happened?" Val asked, looking around and noticing a car about to be towed away and crime scene tape blowing in the wind.

"Somebody killed Bubbles girl, right there in her car." Peaches pointed in the direction of the car being loaded onto a flat bed.

"What, why?" she asked full of confusion and sorrow.

"I don't know, the police wouldn't say shit. All I know, is when I was taking my cigarette break, I heard a lady scream, and when I looked to see what happened, a lot of people were standing around her car, so I made my way over there and saw her in there slumped over dead. Somebody must've already called the police because they were here in a matter of minutes asking questions, but nobody said shit because know body know shit," Peaches exclaimed.

"That's fucked up," Val said shaking her head. "Can we go in or did they shut us down for the day?" she continued after a brief pause.

"They did at first, but we can go back in now," Peaches said before they turned and started walking toward the entrance. Peaches looked back over her shoulder as the tow truck was leaving the parking lot and she shook her head thinking, *Another day in the life of Milwaukee.* Then, she followed Val into the building and back into the dressing room. "You know, it's gettin' real fucked up here," she added seriously.

"Girl it's fucked everywhere," Val said as she disrobed and put on her G-string and bra that was made out of candy.

"True that, I see you goin' all out tonight," she complimented Val's edible garments.

"Gotta catch me a big fish, hook, line, and sinker." They both laughed. "Do you think muthafuckas still coming through tonight after what happened? You know don't nobody wanna be nowhere the police gon' be," Val continued.

"Girl, niggas will travel around the globe and back again for some pussy, so they comin' alright and with a pocket full of money because we do shit they bitches can't do, especially this," Peaches said, leaning against the wall, lifting one of her legs, and putting it behind her head.

"Yeah, that'll get 'em every time," Val smiled.

The club's crowd started to get thicker with a few small time hustlers, some Johns, and a couple lame azz niggas who would ask for lap dances, then try to bargain the price. Then you had players and lesbians who enjoyed the sight of butt naked women and didn't mind paying to see it, but for the most part it was getting filled with some of Milwaukee's best.

"Well I guess it's just gon' be us tonight."

"Ain't no other dancers comin' in?" Val asked curiously.

"You know them tramps comin' in, but I'm talkin' about bitches that's gon' bring in that rent money with one dance."

"You ain't lying about that," Val agreed while adjusting her bra and thong. "Now let's get out here and see what these pockets lookin' like," she added. Walking through the curtains all you could see was ass and titties jiggling as white girl Valerie pranced across the dimly lit club on her way to the stage.

Once she got there, she gave the DJ his cue and then "Bands on You" by Parti Boi and N8 Official bumped loudly out of the speakers. Val started slow winding her hips as several dudes left the dancers at their table, so they could come over and watch the main event.

As Val was on the stage doing her thing, she noticed Chauncey a couple tables away from the stage enjoying the show. *Damn, this muthafucka showed up. There goes my plan, but I knew his azz was gon' be here,* she thought to herself as she licked her finger, ran it in between her legs, and motioned for him to come over there with the other hand.

He smirked, stood up, ran his hand over the front of his shirt, and looked around the room like he was a certified boss before he made his way to the end of the stage and threw his arms out as if to say "What up." Val turned around, dropped to her knees, backed up to the edge of the stage, and when she looked over her shoulder, she wasn't surprised to see that he had all of his attention focused on her ass. She put her cheeks to work and made 'em jump. Left cheek, right cheek, left cheek, right cheek,r ight, right, left. Completely hypnotizing him. Then, she bent backwards, wrapped her arms around his neck, and seductively whispered in his ear, "Yo sexy azz wanna ram yo dick in this tonight?" while biting his ear and boosting his ego sky high.

Val knew in her head that he was locked in a sexual trance and ready to do anything she wanted him to do. She stood up slowly with her ass inches from his face, pulled her thong out and let him eat some of the candies from it.

All the attention Val was giving Chauncey made some of the other dudes in the club jealous, so they started throwing plenty of money on the stage for Val hoping to get a bite of her candy thong or bra. One dude stood holding a couple thousand dollars in singles, threw it onto the stage and yelled.

"This how I do it, it's nothin'," he tried to jack on Chauncey in front of Val. Chauncey dug in his pocket, pulled out eight gees all hundreds, and tossed it on stage to Val. When dude didn't have any more money to throw, Chauncey mugged him, and walked off. Chauncey looked back to Val to see if he'd get some type of confirmation from her that he was the man after throwing all that money, but she stayed focused like the seasoned vet she was. Never would she allow a man who showered her with money believe any amount was enough, she could always use some more.

As Val danced the next song, she looked through the crowd and didn't see Chauncey in sight anymore. Paranoid that she had lost him, as soon as the song went off, she scooped up her earnings, and left the stage in search of Chauncey. She weaved her way through the crowd when she felt a tug on her arm, she turned around and stood face to face with Chauncey.

"I was wondering where you disappeared to, I thought I lost you," she said, relieved that he was still around.

"Naw, I just had to drop somethin' off to one of my homeboys in the parking lot before I head outta town tonight."

"You goin' outta town?" she faked disappointment.

"Yeah, shit gettin' too hot right now, so I gotta duck off for a minute," he replied, but he was taken back by what she said next.

"So, I take it you came here to see if you can stretch this pussy out before you get up outta here, huh?"

"Why you say that?" This made Val wanna reach up and slap the shit outta him for playing with her because they both knew what he wanted to, but she played it cool.

"I figured you liked what you seen over there, soo..." she directed her eyes toward the stage.

"You did yo thang over there, so when can we get it crackin'? You know, let me change yo life," he said while easing his hands on her hips and pulling her closer.

"I think it's the other way around, I'mma change yo life." She held back her smile knowing Richie Rich had something in store for him.

"You think so?"

"I know so," she stated as she slowly removed his hands that were threatening to grip her butt as she walked backwards.

"Where you goin'?" he yelled over the loud music.

"I'll be right back so don't go nowhere," she responded before turning around and disappearing behind the curtain out of sight. Val quickly went to her locker, grabbed her cellphone, and dialed a number. She had a huge grin on her face knowing she was about to do some devilish shit for the first time and prove to Richie Rich that she was down for him in any way he needed her to be. She impatiently waited while the phone rung until he answered.

"Who dis?"

"It's me, I got dude here right now and he ready to leave wit me, so I'm on my way now."

"Aight, you ain't mention my name did you?"

"Come on now, you told me not to. What you think I'mma dumb bitch or somethin'?"

"Who you raisin' yo voice at?" he paused. "Just be on yo way, and when you get here, tell him you gotta call to make sure yo sister don't have the chain on the door. I'mma leave the key in a soda can by the bushes, so you'll see it."

"I'm leaving now and make sure you got my money please."

"I got you," he assured her. "Make sure you park in the back and use the back door," he added.

"Alright, I'll see you when I get there," she said and hung up. Val dressed quickly before she looked in the mirror and told herself, "Let's get this money girl." Grabbing her purse, she made her way back to the main floor and smiled when she found Chauncey waiting there like a trained dog. He returned the smile and held his hand out as she walked up.

"You ready to get outta here?"

"I am if you are," she said as they made their way toward the exit until they were abruptly stopped.

"Girl where you goin'?" Peaches said being her nosey self.

"I'll be back later," she replied as Peaches got the drift.

"Take me wit y'all and we can get it poppin', three is definitely not a crowd wit me," Peaches said seductively, letting them know she was down for whatever. As much as Chauncey wanted to go for the ménage trois offer, he needed to have all his energy and stamina for the white bitch because he was trying to blow her mind so that he could cuff her.

"Not tonight Peaches, me and her got business to attend to, but next time it's a go," he said while passing her a $100 dollar bill and palming a hand full of her ass to make sure she stayed interested.

"It's cool, I'll catch the money train next time, y'all just don't forget about me," she said before she walked off.

"As we were," Chauncey said in a suave type voice while pointing toward the door. Val wanted to burst out laughing at him. 'His lame azz better be lucky he got some money and these T.H.O.T's be liquored up because if it was up to his looks and game, he'd be jagging his dick off every single night.' she thought to herself while maintaining her calm composure.

"I hope you know what you're doing," she said while they walked to his car.

"Absolutely, I slang that Oscar Meyer," he assured her.

"Not just that, I hope I can get some tongue action too. You ballers always want y'all dicks and balls sucked on, but y'all don't wanna eat no pussy."

"Listen, I eat the pussy, lick the ass, suck toes, and I got a big dick so I guarantee you it's going down."

"I hope so," she said replaying Richie Rich's words in her head about it not making it that far. "I'm trippin', you gon' have to follow me to my house because I drove my car," she added.

"That's fine because I'm hittin' the road as soon as I leave your place," he told her before she walked in the direction where her car was parked. Getting in, she looked through her passenger window at Chauncey as he hopped in his 2015 four door Mercedes Benz and started it. Val pulled up on the side of him and motioned for him to let down his window.

"Follow me and you better keep up," she smiled, then sped off through the parking lot and dipped into traffic with him hot on her trail. She looked through her rearview mirror at him. *'I don't know what Richie Rich got planned for him, but whatever it is, he won't see it coming because he's blinded by pussy,* she thought to herself while making a left at the light.

CHAPTER SIXTEEN

*P*ulling into the alley in back of the apartment building, Val parked and watched as Chauncey pulled up and parked.

When she stepped out of the car into the semi-lit alley, she started walking toward the door, and noticed he was still in the car. She smiled and waved her hand motioning for him to come on.

Chauncey slowly got out looking every which way. He cursed himself for not having his gun on him, but he was leaving out of town and didn't plan on making this type of stop before then. Val watched him peeping the scene and noticed that his survival tactics were in full swing. She had to do something to put him at ease, so he wouldn't suspect anything, but first she needed to get the key.

Val quickly made her way to the door and looked off to the side to see a used soda can leaned up against the building, she bent down to retrieve the can, turned it upside down, shook it until the key fell into the palm of her hand, then she threw the can back down.

She looked over to Chauncey who was slowly approaching the building cautiously looking in every direction, so she used that time to ease his mind.

"Come on daddy, you good. I ain't gon' bite unless you want me to," she flirted.

"You sure you don't wanna go to a telly?" he asked.

"We already here and only minutes away from you puttin' this inside of me," she stepped close to him and grabbed his dick through his jeans making him forget about everything else and think with his little head.

"If you say so," he smiled as she pulled out her cellphone. "Who you callin'?" he added.

"I'm calling inside the house to make sure my sister don't have the chain on the door, so we can get in," she said nonchalantly while placing the phone to her ear.

"I thought you lived by yourself?"

"Not until next month," she put up a finger to stop him before he responded. "Girl you got the chain on the door because I'm on my way up....Oh, you ain't home, stay gone then bitch..Aight bye," she laughed while ending the call playing her role to the "T." Val put her phone up and turned toward Chauncey. "Come on, she ain't even here," she added while running her finger down his stomach, stopping at the top of his pants pretending to look inside before she playfully said. "I hope you got something down there for me." Then, she turned around and pushed her butt into his crotch area while opening the door. Chauncey reached down and palmed her plentiful ass while visualizing his dick ramming inside of her thick set of cheeks as they stepped inside the building.

Val knew she had him by the string now, so she looked over her shoulder, and threw him a line that he wasted no biting.

"We fuck around and get it crackin' right here."

"Shit, I'll pull this muthafucka out right now, on my Mama," he said walking step for step with her so his bulge was pressing against her butt. Everything Val was doing gassed him completely up like she was so into him as they made it to

Richie Rich's apartment door. Val pushed him off of her not knowing what to expect when they entered the apartment.

Opening the door, silence took over them as they stared into the dark apartment.

A slight chill ran through Val's body because once they stepped into the apartment, she knew shit was about to get real. Nevertheless, she led him in, shut the door, and used the little light coming through the window to guide him to the let out couch.

"Have a seat on the bed, I'm finna turn some lights on," she said, then walked into the kitchen and turned the lights on, lighting up a good portion of the living room. Once Chauncey seen there was no stick-up kids laying on him, he let out a sigh of relief and got comfortable. He was so keen on taking Val down that he disregarded all possibilities of this being a set up or her even being a threat.

"Y'all just moved in or something?" he asked Val as soon as she returned.

"Yeah, we just got here three months ago from Texas, and we haven't been furniture shopping yet."

"Oh, you from the south? That's why you thicker than grits," he laughed. "When I get back from outta town, I'mma take you to buy whatever you need," he added hoping to persuade her into being with him.

"I guess I should give you an early thank you present," she said reaching around her back, unzipping her dress, and letting it fall to the floor. Chauncey's eyes grew big and his dick threatened to bust outta his pants while looking over Val's luscious body as she began her strip tease.

She sashayed over to him, lifted one of her legs in between his, leaned forward with her mouth open and made ocean like waves with her tongue before seductively licking around her lips. She then opened her leg wider to let him get a glimpse of how fat her lower lips were. Seeing this, Chauncey ran his finger through the crack of her pussy lips, then opened them up exposing her pierced pearl tongue. This turned him on super hard, and with one more look at Val's sexy azz, Chauncey dove in face first and attacked her clitoris with a vicious tongue lashing causing her to moan. He was so lost in the sexual trance sucking, biting, nibbling, and licking her pussy that he didn't even notice Richie Rich come out of the bathroom in the crouching position and duck walk into the living room.

As Richie Rich got closer, Val seen him out of her peripheral, but she never broke her routine. She grabbed the back of Chauncey's head and pushed it deep into her pussy while moaning louder until Richie Rich got close enough.

Pushing Chauncey back on the bed, Val unbuckled his pants, then pulled them and his boxers down to his ankles. Chauncey closed his eyes preparing for her hot mouth when she grabbed his member, but instead of a mouth, he felt a big piece of cold steel pressed against the side of his face. He quickly opened his eyes to see Val backing away slowly.

"You punk azz bitch," he said to her knowing what time it was. Then, he turned his head only to meet with the most horrifying, blood shot red, enraged pair of eyes that he had ever seen.

"What up bitch azz nigga? You thought I was dead, didn't you?" Richie Rich growled in a low tone before slapping him with the pistol. "Well you always been a stupid muthafucka," he added.

"What the...." Chauncey said while holding his jaw as he tried to get up hoping his eyes were deceiving him.

"Move again and I'mma push yo shit back," he said now standing over him with his gun still pointed at his head. Chauncey looked over at Val and couldn't believe he fell for the okey doke. He told himself that if he lived, she was a dead bitch.

"Nigga I trusted you and what you do? You killed my brother, my woman, and my unborn child, and you tried to kill me," he paused. Val stood off to the side shocked by Richie Rich's revelations, but she already felt that Chauncey had something to do with him being shot. "Then on top of that, you stole my dope, my money, and you got the nerve to be runnin' round here splurgin' wit my shit like you put the work in to make it to where I did, knowing you was a bum azz nigga before I started fuckin' wit you," Richie Rich continued. "You can love the game, but that bitch don't love nobody back, now get yo bitch azz over there," he added before slapping him across the head with the pistol causing him to roll out of the bed and onto the floor.

"Karma's a bitch ain't it?" Richie Rich said while kicking Chauncey as he slid up against the wall. "Tie that nigga up," he said pointing the gun toward Val.

"With what?" she asked nervously.

"I don't know, use the nigga shoe strings."

Val quickly started taking the laces from the new Lebron's he was wearing before figuring that they might not work."I don't think these gon' be long enough," she turned toward Richie Rich.

"Well go in the kitchen, get a knife, and cut the TV cord or somethin'. Damn bitch, just tie 'em up, fuck!" he said in pure frustration while keeping his gun pointed on his old friend. Chauncey just sat there in disbelief that Richie Rich was still alive and kicking when he could've sworn that he hit him in the heart, but obviously he couldn't have. Chauncey looked up from his thoughts at Richie Rich and he could see from the look in his eyes, that death wasn't far away for him.

"I been impatiently waiting to catch yo azz...shit, I already knew you was a sucka for some pussy, so I played on your weakness knowing you was bound to slip, but you definitely wasn't the only one. I hollered at yo cousin Clyde too."

Chauncey's face told a helluva story and that was evident by the expression on it. "I knew I should have been left up outta town after everybody started coming up missin'," he mumbled under his breath as Richie Rich rambled on.

"I hollered at yo boy Schod. He was flexin' too much on the gram, led me right to him. I caught up wit Bubbles trifling azz too." Val looked up in shock because she had no idea that he killed Bubbles, but she stayed composed and kept tying Chauncey up while thinking she may have bit off more than she could chew because Richie Rich was nothing but a killer as far as she was concerned.

"I ain't have to worry about dealing with Gunna because the streets dealt with his shiesty azz, and that bitch Jazzie got did in by the law, and just how they all met their fate, you'll soon meet yours."

"You just runnin' yo fuckin' mouth, you don't know what the fuck you talkin' bout," Chauncey said but deep down in his gut, he knew the pieces of the puzzle he was missing fell right into place when Richie gave them to him.

"You done yet?"

"Finished," she said jumping up and looking at Richie Rich for further instructions.

"Put yo clothes on and get back to the club, I'mma call you later and don't be runnin' yo mouth about shit that went down here."

"I ain't," she said while sliding her dress and heels on before heading to the door, then she turned back around. "Oh yeah, what about my money?"

Richie Rich bent down, picked up Chauncey's pants, dug inside his pocket, and pulled out a set of keys and what he estimated to be about 6 or 7 gees in two rubberbanded knots. He tossed her both of the knots and shook his head when she didn't catch 'em.

"Call me," she said stuffing the money inside of her purse before leaving out of the door.

Richie Rich walked over to Chauncey and kicked him so hard in the mouth that he knocked his front four teeth out.

"You punk azz muthafucka," he said in an angry shrill. "You betrayed me in the worst way, you took my brother...BAM! Jamillah...BAM! and my baby." BAM! BAM!

Richie Rich slapped him with the pistol over and over until Chauncey was barely maintaining his breathing as blood bubbles and slob ran from his mouth.

Richie went into the kitchen and grabbed a roll of duct tape, came back, and ran it around Chauncey's mouth while going around his head every time.

"Get yo bitch azz up," he said grabbing him by the neck, forcing him to stand up. "Let's go for a ride," he added. Richie Rich guided him toward the door then rammed his face into it.

"Fuck," Chauncey mumbled in pain.

Opening the door, Richie Rich looked out to see nobody coming from either direction, so he pushed a butt naked

Chauncey out into the hallway and made him fall by the backdoor, then he kicked him in the ass.

"Get the fuck up," he kicked him again before reaching down to pull him up by the back of his neck. Richie Rich looked out of the back door to the apartment into the cool night air as the wind blew the leaves and potato chip bags up and down the alley, but there was not a soul outside.

"Let's go," he pushed Chauncey down the one step by the backdoor causing him to fall again and scrape his knee. Chauncey let out a muffled scream and tried to grab his knee.

"Yo bitch azz aight," Richie Rich said digging into his pocket, getting the keys he took from Chauncey's pocket, and then hitting the alarm. When he seen what car's headlights blink, he said, "Oh, you got a Benz? Did I buy that for you? You would've never got that without me."

Richie Rich led Chauncey to the Benz, opened the trunk, and when he tried to push him in, Chauncey tried to resist. Richie Rich put the gun in his waistband, punched him in the gut, kneed him in the nuts, then pushed him in the trunk, and reached over and put his legs in.

Chauncey laid in the trunk butt naked and cold staring at his old friend with a regretful look on his face knowing he would soon come to an end and there was nothing he could do about it.

"Don't look so pitiful, you should've thought about that before you took what was most important to me." And with that, Richie Rich hit in the jaw so hard that it knocked him out. Then as he looked in the trunk for something to bust the trunk light, he spotted a small duffel bag, he pulled that out, busted the light with a screwdriver, closed the trunk and hopped behind the wheel. Unzipping the bag, he smiled, threw it on the passenger seat, started the car, and pulled off.

*****

"Damn bitch that was fast," Peaches said walking over to Val. "Where he at?" she added.

"Girl you know how dudes get after they get a nut, they be sleeping like new born babies." Val played her part while laughing and looking at Peaches noticing the hate in her eyes.

"Bitch please, you ain't got it like that."

Val realized that Peaches was on some bullshit, but not wanting to play into her hands, Val politely gave it to her with no cut.

"That hatin' you doin' don't even look good on you. I promise you it don't. Besides you act like you new to this shit. I ain't finna lay wit the dude,I'mma let him dip his stick in this sauce, he bust, I'm in the wind, he is not my dude," Val stated, "But look what a little fun time did get me," she opened her purse and tilted it so Peaches could get a peek.

"Damn bitch I told you I wanted in, but yo selfish azz wanted him all to yourself," Peaches said with envy after seeing her banded up.

"Naw, he wanted me all to himself, get it right."

"I'm tryna get this money too."

"I'll tell you what, let's dip off in the back and I'll give you $500 to suck on my pussy for ten minutes straight."

Peaches' jaw dropped in aww. "What!? Bitch you cra..." she started but was cut off.

"That's what I'm talking about, you talk a good game, but you not bout that action. You ain't willing to do what it takes, it ain't no rules to this shit. If you give me $500 right now, I'll suck yo pussy and make you cum twice, and if you think I'm lying put the money up," Val said looking Peaches directly in the eyes.

Looking around in shock, Peaches couldn't believe Val was approaching her with this kind of proposition. She stared at her while shaking her head before she spoke.

"I should call you on it."

"Give me the money, take yo thong off, lay back, and see if I'm playing then."

"Naw I'm good," Peaches said after thinking about it. But she did recognize that Val was about that go-getta life.

"Well let's get out here and get this money," Val looked out the curtains to see some potential vics. Then she slapped Peaches on the ass hard and walked out into the crowded club.

Peaches grabbed her butt and noticed Val's handprint. "This bitch got fucked and went crazy," she said to herself then she made her way to the main floor.

CHAPTER SEVENTEEN

*C*hauncey had just awoken as Richie Rich brought the car to a stop. He tried his best to listen to see if he could pinpoint his location, but he had the slightest idea because he couldn't hear nothing. He knew Richie Rich was a calculated nigga, so wherever they were, it was secluded.

Suddenly the car door opened, and footsteps traced alongside of the car until they stopped directly at the back. The trunk swung up and there was Richie Rich looking down upon him laying there cold, naked, and vulnerable. Chauncey could see that he had vengeance in his eyes as he reached in the trunk, grabbed him by the neck in an attempt to make him sit up. But Chauncey was six feet tall, so the trunk was too little for him to sit up in, so he leaned on his side ,then Richie Rich used his gloved hand to yank the tape from around his mouth.

"What you gotta say for yourself?"

"Man you gotta understand my situat..." he started, but Richie changed his mind about hearing what he had to say.

"Just shut the fuck up,I'ont even wanna hear that shit."

"You already got yo mind up, so it ain't shit I can say," he rambled on while looking around realizing he was in Washington Park behind the pavilion. Richie Rich disregarded his frivolous chatter as he walked to the passenger's door, grabbed the duffel bag and put it around him diagonally, then he opened the back door and grabbed the gasoline can. Shutting both doors, he walked back to the trunk, and sat it on the ground.

When he stood up, he pulled out his .45 caliber automatic pistol, crossed his arms, and stood there in silence staring at his so called friend. At this point Chauncey knew there was nothing he could do that would save his life, so he decided to unleash a verbal assault on him to comfort his pride.

"Fuck you then bitch azz nigga,y ou's a hoe and you always gon' be one, you and yo hoe azz brother, that's why he dead now. He did all he could for yo stupid azz to accept him, but you was too busy dick ridin' me to see what he had to offer, wit yo gay azz. I should've let dude kill yo bitch azz in that alley. And you call yo self a playa, fallin' in love wit that hoe bitch, that's why she dead too, and fuck yo baby too, FUCK YO KIDS NIGGA! YOU A HOE. I KNOW,YOU KNOW! AND IF YOU UNTIE ME, I'LL BEAT YO BITCH AZZ RIGHT NOW!" he screamed getting amped up. Once Richie Rich calmly bent down and picked up the gasoline can, his treats turned into pleading sobs.

"I'm sorry bro, I swear, I don't know what the fuck came over me, I don't wanna die cuz, please,"he cried, but Richie Rich had heard enough as he started to douse him and the interior of the trunk in gasoline, then he sat the can back down calmly, and pointed the gun at Chauncey. BOC! He shot him in the shoulder, the gunshot echoed throughout the park.

"Yo bitch azz bet not eva say no shit like that about my family, fuck yo kids too nigga."

"Arrghh," Chauncey moaned out in agony when the hollow tip bullet started to expand in his shoulder. Richie had enough, it was time to put an end to this ordeal.

"In this case, it's three ways to be the light, be the candle, the mirror that reflects it, or you could be you," he said tucking the pistol away, then he pulled out the rag and set a flame to it.

"Huh?"Chauncey asked puzzled

"I'll see you in hell faggot azz Chauncey."he said and tossed the lit rag into the trunk. Chauncey tried to hop and scoot but to no avail because him and the trunk were coated in gasoline 'POOF' the flame went ablaze.

Richie Rich jumped back as Chauncey screamed while his flesh slowly burned and peeled from his body. The TV cords burned off immediately as he continued to hop around like a fish outta water. When he made an attempt to get out of the trunk, Richie Rich quickly pulled out the .45 and shot him five times. BOC! BOC! BOC! BOC! BOC! The last shot hit him directly in the head and made him fall back into the trunk.

Richie Rich stood there for a minute watching him burn to a crisp. Coming to his senses, he looked around to see if anyone had witnessed what he had just done, seeing nobody insight, he picked up the gasoline can and finished dousing the interior of the car before throwing the remainder in the car. Then he got outta there just in time as the flames became engulfed.

Richie Rich started to jog in the direction of his house on 39th and Garfield which was about five blocks from the park so he could dump the money, hop in the stoley, and go take care of some other business he had to take care of.

*****

"I know this bitch didn't, "Val said fumbling through her purse before she threw it back into her locker, slammed the door, and made her way outta the locker room, but Peaches was already coming through the curtain counting money from her last few lap and table dances.

"What up girl?"

"Bitch don't what up me, where the fuck my money at!?"Val barked.

"I don't know, fuck you askin' me for?" Peaches shot back feeling offended, but she played it cool and tried to walk off, but Val grabbed her by the shoulder.

"Bitch I ain't playin' wit you!" she yelled so loud that it echoed throughout the small locker room as she started removing her earrings ready for fisticuffs.

"I know you beta get the fuck out my face," Peaches said then, proceeded to walk away, when Val suddenly rushed her and pinned her up against the wall with her face so close that their noses were touching.

"You betta give me my fuckin' money," she said as spit was flying out of her mouth onto Peaches.

"Get the fuck off me, I said I ain't got yo shit, you betta ask one of them other hoes," she said turning her head to the side to avoid the spit.

"It's funny how I just showed you my money, now my shit missin', I ain't goin' for that, and I tell you what," she walked over to her locker, opened it, unzipped her purse, and pulled out a small switchblade. "I'mma get my shit one way or another," she added.

"So, you gon' pull a knife out on me bitch?"

"Give..Me..My..Money," Val said, putting emphasis on each word.

"I ain't got time for this shit," Peaches said, leaving out of the Locker room with Val hot on her ass. She rounded a few tables, then passed P.T. as he was sitting at the bar with his old school pimp buddy Yellow from Chicago.

"Where y'all goin'?" he asked noticing Peaches and Val heading out the door in their stripper costumes which he didn't allow.

"I'm just going outside to get some fresh air, that's all," Peaches said while still in motion. P.T. noticed Val seconds behind her and figured it must've been an altercation between the two, he shook his head, sipped his drink, and said.

"Them hoes gon' work it out."

"Sure will, you know how bitches get," Yellow said as the shared a laugh.

Peaches made it outside and walked to the side of the building to light a cigarette and get Val off of her mind.

Richie Rich pulled up outside of the strip club and turned his lights off. He saw Val's car and knew she was still inside, so he'd wait on her to come out because he didn't wanna be seen.

About five minutes later, he saw Peaches come out of the club into the cool summer night wearing only a bra, boy shorts, and a pair of heels. She seems to be in a rush and that alerted Richie Rich that something was up because she never left the club for nothing.

He sat up when he seen the door swing open again and Val come out of the club looking in both directions. Although it was a little distance between them, he could still see that she had something shinny in her hand, but he wasn't sure what it was as she followed in Peaches' direction.

Val walked up on Peaches who was standing on the side of the building alone smoking a cigarette and started swinging her hand with the shiny object from side to side.

After seeing this, Richie Rich was pretty sure that the object in her hand was a knife, so he sat back and lowered the window so he could hear what was going on.

"I know you ain't think this shit was over," Val said then lunged toward Peaches' face with the knife.

"Bitch you bet not stab me wit that knife," Peaches said after side stepping the attempted plunge to the face.

"If I do, what you gon' do about it?" Val replied while walking up toward her. But before she could raise the knife, Peaches pushed her hard enough that she stumbled back on her high heels and almost fell. "No you didn't!" she continued after regaining her balance. Then in one swift motion she jumped up, pushed Peaches against the building, and pushed the blade inside of her torso. "Where my shit at bitch? I told you not to fuck wit me," she added in a low growl as Peaches reached down trying to pull the knife out.

"I ain't...go...yo..." was all Peaches could muster as she took her last gasp of air before she collapsed to the pavement.

Once Val's anger and adrenaline finally subsided, she looked down at Peaches and realized that she was dead. She threw the knife down, and put her hands over her mouth and said.

"Oh my god!"

CHAPTER EIGHTEEN

A distraught Val stood there looking down at Peaches' slumped over dead body while crying her eyes out when she heard somebody calling her name. She turned to a silhouette appear in the parking lot next to an unfamiliar car.

Confused and shocked, she tried to focus in on the person who was calling her name, but everything seemed so blurry to her, then she figured she knew whoever it was because they were calling her name, so she pulled herself together, snapped back to her senses, and staggered over to where the person was who was calling her because she knew that she was in no shape to go back in the club. She hoped whoever it was could offer her some aid and assistance.

Val started sobbing and crying again as she was getting closer to who was calling he, so he rushed over to help her quickly get to the car, once he seen there was nobody else outside of the club.

"What was that all about?" Richie Rich asked while he directed her to the passenger side of the car.

"That bitch stole my money," she said now knowing who was calling her name. "What are you doing here?" she added

"Remember I told you I was gonna get up wit you later. I called and you didn't answer so I figured you'd be here. Now get in and let's get the fuck outta here before somebody see's us." he stated as she got in the car. He shut the door, rushed around to the driver's side, and got in just as two people were walking out of the club.

Richie Rich leaned back in his seat and watched the two people carry on with a normal conversation followed by laughter, then they stumbled their way to their car not even going in the direction where they would've found Peaches laying there dead. Once they pulled out and left, Richie Rich did the same thing.

"Who all know you and her came outside together?" he asked curiously.

"Nobody I think."

"You think? You need to know bitch!" he barked while making a right on Villard.

"Nobody, I'm sure," she said, not thinking straight. "What happened to 'ol boy Chauncey?" she added.

"I just fucked him over a lil bit and left him in the park butt naked to embarrass him, so he won't ever think about fuckin' me over again," he said while weaving through traffic.

"That's a little light considering he killed your family, tried to kill you, and you killed everybody else he fucked with," she stated. Richie Rich didn't say a word. He knew the white bitch knew too much information. Knowing this, he just pressed the gas pedal a little harder.

"Where we bout to go?" she asked, still shaken up about committing a murder.

"To this little duck off spot so we can clear our heads and plan our next move."

"I ain't got time to clear my head, I just killed somebody Richie," she said with her voice cracking, letting him know that tears were only seconds away.

"Here" he reached in the ashtray and handed her a fat blunt of loud. "That should ease your mind a little bit." he added before looking in his rearview mirror to make sure the cops weren't on them.

Val lit the blunt and took a long hard puff before she started coughing hard, then she leaned back in her seat, and closed her eyes. Richie Rich watched her take puff after puff out the corner of his eye and he could tell that she was becoming relaxed as the potent weed started to take care of her worries and concerns.

Val took a few more puffs, passed it to Richie who took a couple long puffs, blew the smoke out of his nose, passed it back to her, and said, "Kill it," as he reached Villard and Green Bay Avenue, turned, pulled into the basketball courts parking lot at Meaux Park otherwise known as Lincoln Park.

Richie Rich pulled closer to the back so that when he turned his headlights off, the car couldn't be seen from the main street. He turned the engine off and hit a couple notches on the volume to 'Betrayed' by Lil Boosie & Webbie as he collected his thoughts, then he decided it was time to see where her head was.

"I could seriously fuck wit a bitch like you," he looked over to her. Val just leaned against the window high as hell and lost in deep thought, so all his words sounded like blah blah blah to her because all she could think about was how she rammed that knife inside of Peaches. Although it had only been 10 or 15 minutes, her conscious was eating her alive and she couldn't help but to imagine how she was going to get away with it.

"I should turn myself in, this ain't right," she broke the silence.

"You don't wanna do that," he said while thinking she wasn't as thorough as he initially thought, so he pressed the issue to see how she would react. "So what we gon' do about this? because I gotta trust you to keep yo mouth closed, so goin' to the police ain't even an option!" he added sternly, but all she heard him say was.

"We gon' do this...I trust you," as she turned and faced the window with her eyes closed, she was trippin' hard off the murder and the weed.

"Did you hear me?"

"Yeah I heard you. You said you trust me, right?" she turned back toward him and when she opened her eyes, she was staring down the barrel of his .45 caliber pistol. BOC!

He pulled the trigger and the right side of her face exploded, splashing blood on the dashboard and onto the bullet shattered window before her body slumped back into the seat.

Richie Rich had to take her out because she knew too much and she was becoming more and more reckless by the minute and he couldn't afford to have any loose ends. If he was gonna play the game, he had to play it by the code, because if he was gon' LIVE BY IT, he was prepared to DIE BY IT if he had too.

THE END

(but it's only the beginning!)

Also Available by Bagz of Money Content

1. Live by It, Die by It (By: Ice Money)
2. Mercenary (By: Ice Money)
3. The Ruler of the Red Ruler (By: Kutta)
4. Block Boyz (By: Juve)
5. Team Savage (By Ace Boogie)
6. Team Savage 2 (By Ace Boogie)

Available at Bagzofmoneycontent.com and most major bookstores.